AFRICAN PASSIONS

AND

OTHER STORIES

BEATRIZ RIVERA

Arte Público Press
Houston, Texas
1995

This volume is made possible through grants from the National Endowment for the Arts (a federal agency), the Lila Wallace-Reader's Digest Fund, and the Andrew W. Mellon

Recovering the past, creating the future

Arte Público Press
University of Houston
Houston, Texas 77204-2090

humca

Cover design by Mark Piñón
Original art by Benito Huerta

Rivera, Beatriz, 1957–
    African passions and other stories / by Beatriz Rivera.
        p.   cm.
    ISBN 1-55885-135-6
    I. Title.
PS3568.I8287A69   1995
813'.54—dc20   94-36017
                                                   CIP

The paper used in this publication meets the requirements of the American National Standard for Permanence of Paper for Printed Library Materials Z39.48-1984. ∞

ACKNOWLEDGEMENTS

"African Passions" first appeared in *The Bilingual Review*, 1995.

"Life Insurance" first appeared in *Chiricú*, Vol. 6, No. 3, 1992, pp. 29–41.

"Paloma" first appeared in *The Americas Review*, Vol. 20, No. 2, 1992, pp. 15–30.

For my parents,
Mario Rivera and Aida Rivera,
with love and respect.

CONTENTS

AFRICAN PASSIONS 9

LIFE INSURANCE 22

WHAT MIRANDA LOST 34

ONCE IN A LIFETIME OFFERING 57

BELLS 86

THE BATTERY-OPERATED DRUMMER BEAR 115

GRANDMOTHER'S SECRET 139

PALOMA 150

African Passions

and

Other Stories

AFRICAN PASSIONS

So he was awake. If not, he wouldn't have held his breath when she touched him. Anyway, sleeping people do tend to look more natural. Armando was just making a big effort to keep his eyes shut, tightly wrinkled shut, so she wouldn't bother him. Teresa could tell. He was on the alert, as if she were an ugly brown bear ready to pounce if he didn't play dead.

"Are you asleep, love?" she asked, because maybe, just maybe, she was wrong, and he was just hassled, not hassled by her, just hassled.

He groaned, his jaw muscle twitched, he continued faking sleep. Gently, Teresa stroked his chest. Torn between sadness and anger, she tried again.

"Do you still love me?" she asked.

Then she tried again. "Is anything wrong?" Still no response.

"Armando! Armando!" she insisted.

"Huh?" He pretended to be startled.

"Armando, if you don't pay attention to me soon, I'll do something crazy!" she threatened half-jokingly.

Armando let out a fake "huh?" again and continued playing dead.

"Something really crazy," she insisted.

"African Powers that surround our Savior," she prayed to herself. "Don't say I didn't warn you, Armando," she said out loud. "African Powers that surround our Savior," she repeated to herself.

It wasn't that Teresa really believed in Santería. In any case, that's what she said. The main argument was that she lived on the Upper East Side of Manhattan where there were gourmet delis instead of live poultry markets and those religious stores called *Botánicas*. And it had been years since she'd belonged to the old neighborhood. Santería was simply her private game, the way she liked to pray when she really wanted something.

"African Powers that surround our Savior: Eleggua, Ogún, Obatalá, Shangó, Yemayá, Oshún, Orula, Babalú Ayé. I want pleasure! And I want it right away!"

Immediately, the cat jumped on the bed and started walking all over her, demanding to be fed. And since Teresa did summon the African Powers, they came.

Babalú Ayé was the first. He emerged from the corn, in a foul mood because Teresa had summoned him last. And besides, he didn't like her tone of voice; it was too arrogant. He waited for Eleggua to creep out from underneath the sugar bowl where he lived, then started saying mean things about Teresa. Why did she have a cat instead of a dog, for instance. Babalú loved dogs; they had soft tongues. And since Babalú's body was covered with open wounds, a cat's rough tongue just wouldn't do. And wasn't Teresa the one who had once said that she'd always have everything she wanted? Well, she never did get Armando to marry her, even if Eleggua was bent over backwards for her. Eleggua had always opened all roads for Teresa, but Babalú said he wasn't in the least bit impressed. He made fun of Teresa for having written Hispanic on every single dotted line and managed to get into top universities, top law firms, and top floors. "But even if she's a partner and real successful and making lots of money, Armando still won't marry her!" Babalú bragged. "Who cares if they've even nicknamed her the Doberman for defending South American interests so well here in North America?! Eleggua, are you listening?" No, he wasn't. Eleggua smelled leftover chicken in the refrigerator and was dying to eat it. That's why he made the cat heavier, louder, more insistent.

"Why don't you go and feed that cat?" moaned Armando.

"O.K., O.K., patience, Gato, sweetness, love cat, wait, I'll feed you," Teresa said. Wobbly, she got out of bed, stretched her back and slipped into a robe. "Yes, sweetness, kitten, last night's chicken, you want that?"

The spice rack trembled in the kitchen and out of the pepper jumped Orula, the clairvoyant. Then the bloodthirsty Ogún crawled out of the rosemary, and the feminine Yemayá flew out of the cilantro. Shangó, who loves fire, came from the bay leaves, and the virile warrior Obatalá from the marjoram. Babalú Aye kept asking everyone if they didn't find it shocking that Teresa had summoned him last. "What nerve she has!"

"Yes, Gato, sweet cat, and you want to eat on the window sill? I'll open the window for you, yes. It's a beautiful day today, bright and sunny. Now will you let me go back to bed? Cat, I'm begging!"

Back in the bedroom, Teresa slipped out of her robe and crawled back into bed. She snuggled close to Armando and gently caressed his stomach and thighs and chest. "Do you still love me?" she whispered in his ear. Teresa loved being in bed with him, so close to him. Moments such as these seemed rare even if they'd been together for fourteen years. Most of the time, they were either on business trips or on a very tight schedule. Today, Teresa was so glad that neither of them was rushing off to work or to the airport. She kept snuggling closer and closer to him, wanting him more than anything in the world. But he didn't seem interested. "African Powers, did you hear me?!" That's when, from Teresa's gold jewelry, rose the beautiful party-loving Oshún with a bad case of the giggles. Laughing hard, she asked, "Where's my sister Yemayá?"

"Looking for her husband Orula, as usual," replied Shangó, who had tried to rape Oshún the night before. "What about a once-a-week affair?" Shangó suggested to Oshún. "It would do us both good," he insisted. "Don't cut me, I was just kidding! Look at Orula following Eleggua, his best ally, around. They've already circled the cat ten times!"

Life should have gotten easier, but it just hadn't. In the past few months Teresa had barely seen Armando. Ever since February, she'd spent every single weekend alone, and now it was spring. Unwillingly, for the memory came all by itself, or with the fur that the cat had left on the bed, Teresa thought of the cat's age, fourteen years, and how she'd found that kitten out in the street the day they were moving in together. She was twenty years old, a paralegal in Armando's law firm, applying to law schools. She was doing well in college and had taken so many extra-credit courses that she was almost ready to graduate. And Armando had just become a junior partner. He was thirty. Ten years older. They were supposed to live together, then get married, have babies, and be successful. Eleggua took his eyes off the chicken for a minute and bragged that he was the one who had opened all roads for Teresa. Well, they'd gotten the successful part right, and the

living together part right, and she'd told her parents that they
had eloped, for her parents would have had a fit if they had
known that she was simply living with him. Then once her
parents got over the shock of her supposedly eloping, they
were quite proud of their daughter having found an upper-
crust Cuban, or a "country club" Cuban as her father used to
say. That meant that he would have belonged to one of the
Havana country clubs if Castro hadn't come along. "I only got
to see the inside of those clubs when I got jobs cleaning toilets
there!" José Bos added, proud that his daughter Teresa had
married into the "cream" of Cuba.

Armando was so attracted to her then. And even if his
family didn't quite approve because no matter how successful
and intelligent she was they always saw her as a lower-class
Jersey City, New Jersey, Cuban girl whose family owned a
laundromat, Armando said he didn't care, he adored her, he
couldn't take his hands off her.

Oh, she loved Armando so much! "Te quiero," she whispered in his ear. "I love you. I adore you," she kept repeating
while caressing his thigh, happy that they had a whole weekend together. She'd been looking forward to it. A month ago,
he'd told her to reserve this weekend so they could be
together, and talk. What about? Marriage? Love? Suddenly
she remembered. "What are we supposed to talk about this
weekend, Armando?"

He was still pretending to be asleep. Teresa kissed his
neck and got a whiff of the past again. That time, they had
broken up because he'd met someone else and had even
wanted to marry that *fulanita*. And she started seeing other
men. And he had said he could never marry her. His parents
would never forgive him. His sister would never forgive him.
His aunts would never forgive him. Not that they had anything against her personally. Couldn't she put herself in his
place? What if she brought someone home to meet her parents
and that person just didn't pass? You know…That person
could be a very nice person, and it's not that they'd have anything against that person, they just wouldn't want that person to be part of the family. So it was with his parents. Teresa
just wasn't…What did they say? Of their class. His family was
so hung up on class, and so was Armando, although he pretended not to be so. So they'd broken up, and she started seeing other men. But then he couldn't stand the thought of her

being with other men, so they'd gotten back together again. He still hadn't married her though, probably because she just didn't have that blue blood. And he was always inventing fresh new excuses for not marrying her. It was O.K. She never even nagged him about it. "Don't search for an excuse!" she'd say. "Just promise we'll always be together," she'd laugh.

"Teresita, mi amor, this is serious. I want you to understand," he'd insist. "I just don't believe in marriage," he'd try to explain with a guilty look on his face.

"Armando, all I want is to be with you forever!"

She believed him and respected his decision. After all, they'd been together for fourteen years. In the kitchen, Babalú was pouring sesame seeds on the floor so Teresa would die of gangrene.

"I love you wildly," Teresa murmured again. "And I want you."

Yemayá decided, since it was Saturday, her day, that she'd make Armando have a stomachache. Suddenly, Armando opened his eyes and looked at his watch.

"You don't have any commitments today, do you?" Teresa asked.

"No, just a phone call," he replied. "Will you bring me an Alka-Seltzer, Terry, mi amor?"

That's when Yemayá yelled, "He's got the stomachache!!"

And right after that, the party-and-laughter-loving Oshún, who was blowing the sesame seeds away, cried out, "I'll get his genitals! I love his genitals!"

Oshún was giggling even harder now because she'd destroyed Babalú's jinx and had gotten rid of every single sesame seed.

"Do you want her to hemorrhage?" asked Ogún, who smelled of rosemary.

"She summoned me last!" Babalú replied. "Last! And I'm not one to be joked with," he added.

"Of course I'll get you Alka-Seltzer. You just stay right there. Don't go away!" Teresa answered Armando.

When Teresa returned with the Alka-Seltzer, Armando had his hand on the telephone receiver and an embarrassed look on his face.

"Do you want coffee?" she asked.

"Huh? What? Coffee? Oh, sure!" he said, and took his hand off the receiver because Shangó had made it too hot.

"I feel like burning him," said Shangó.

"And I'll cut him," Ogún added.

"Get Eleggua in here, tell him to slam some doors, Teresa doesn't even realize we're here!" yelled Shangó. "Oshún, Sagrada Puta, why are you on her side?"

"Armando, every time I ask you a question you look so embarrassed! " said Teresa.

"Huh?" was his reaction, and then he looked at his watch again and gulped the Alka-Seltzer down and said, "Thank you for the Alka-Seltzer, mi amor, of course I'd like coffee. This phone call will only take five minutes. Please don't come into the bedroom while I'm talking; you'll just distract me, O.K?"

"I love you, Armando," Teresa said.

"I love you, too. Now let me make this phone call, and then I'll be all yours."

It was a beautiful Saturday morning, and the kitchen window was wide open, and the cat was on the sill eating slowly. This was his favorite spot. It seemed awfully high and dangerous, but cats don't fall. While preparing the coffee, Teresa was loudly singing some boleros.

"Shut that woman up!" Babalú cried out.

"The cat's eating all the chicken!" Orula said to Eleggua.

"I'll help you push him out the window!" said Ogún.

Teresa kept singing loudly.

"And I'll help, too," volunteered Babalú.

"Oh, my God!" Teresa interrupted her singing and yelled all of a sudden.

"We pushed *gato!*" Babalú yelled.

"OhmyGodmyGodmyGod!" Teresa yelled again. "No, it was an optical illusion! African Powers, tell me it was an optical illusion!" She ran to the window and looked down. They were nine floors up, so she couldn't see anything…"OhMyGodOhMyGod," she repeated. "Gato! Gato!!" she began calling for the cat. Had he really fallen out the window? "OhMyGod, did this happen?!"

A few minutes later, while Teresa was still calling the cat, the super buzzed her from downstairs to tell her that poor Gato seemed to have fallen out the window and was dead on the sidewalk, but that he was completely intact, if that was any consolation. Teresa said she'd be right down then ran to the bathroom, splashed water on her face, then burst into the bedroom to get a pair of jeans and a sweatshirt. Armando was sitting up in bed, whispering into the receiver, smiling. When he saw her, his expression changed suddenly; he seemed ashamed of himself. But it probably wasn't shame, just anger because she was disturbing him when he'd told her not to come into the bedroom while he was on the phone. For a minute the thought crossed Teresa's mind that she was getting her signals crossed with Armando's facial expressions. But how could that happen after all these years? she wondered, and at the same time ordered the elevator to hurry. Didn't she know him by heart? Was she reading sex-guilt where there was simply minor irritation due to stress and overwork? But he looked so guilty! And how can you look sex-guilty when you're on the phone talking business?

Teresa was about to really start wondering what was going on when Orula, the clairvoyant, blew the thought away. "Don't let her be prepared for this day!"

The super gave Teresa that warm bundle in a blanket and held the elevator open for her.

Back in the apartment, Teresa wiped the tears off her face with her cuff and called Armando. But he was under the shower.

In the kitchen, Eleggua was stuffing himself with chicken. Teresa put the bundle on one of the chairs then sat down, put her head in her hands, and waited for Armando.

And she must've fallen asleep, maybe for ten minutes, but it seemed so long, he startled her by saying loudly, "Where'd you disappear to?"

"Were you asleep?" he asked. "Where's my coffee? Never mind, I'll get it. God, did I ever cut myself shaving!"

"Armando, the cat fell out the window," she said, and pointed to the bundle on the kitchen chair. "I ran downstairs to get him while you were on the phone."

Armando seemed quite upset. He said he loved that cat, they'd had him for such a long time. Teresa wondered what they should do with him now. Call the ASPCA? Armando suggested they bury him. He's the one who insisted, and yes, she was definitely getting her signals crossed, for he looked sex-guilty even when he said they should take the car and find somewhere in the suburbs to bury that poor cat. Yes, and they'd stop at some hardware store to buy a shovel. They

didn't even have to go that far. Riverdale, for example. Or
Fort Lee, New Jersey. Or even Englewood; they had woods
there. Someplace like that. They'd had this cat for so long
that he certainly deserved a decent burial. "Don't you think
so, Teresita, mi amor?" Armando seemed so ashamed of himself!

"Did you hear that?" asked Eleggua with his mouth full.
"They're taking us for a ride! Put your best clothes on! And
that goes for everyone!"

After Teresa showered, they consulted the map of the
New York area and vicinity. The African Powers were all
ready to go. Teresa kept repeating that they couldn't bury the
cat in a public park or someplace like that. Armando assured
her that they'd find some vacant, woodsy land.

"Certainly not in The Bronx!" Teresa said. "You're pointing to it!"

"Well, further north, like here, Dobbs Ferry. There seems
to be a golf course here."

"So, we're going to bury the cat in a golf course now?"

"Well, what about here? Near Nyack College, see? There's
green there. Oh, no, that's a golf course, too. We need some
government land where we're sure they won't disturb the
grave. Look, anywhere where it says national recreation,
that'll never be touched. What about Robert Moses State Park
here? And they even have a bird sanctuary."

"Do you think we'll be able to stop and dig a hole there?"
Teresa asked.

"Sure! It's probably deserted. So, we'll take the Triborough to Grand Central Parkway. Then, hold it, page 69, yeah,
Northern Boulevard—or is that Northern State? Think
they're the same thing? Can you read what it says there?"

"Sagtikos State. Let's just go, Armando!"

Now they both looked guilty with that baby-sized bundle
in the back seat. "God, this weekend's turning into a funeral,"
Teresa commented.

They drove in silence for a while with a dead cat and all
those African Powers. It wasn't until they were crossing the
Triborough Bridge that the party-loving Oshún, the only one
of the African Powers that wasn't asleep, made Teresa ask,
"What's this about your parents coming to New York next
weekend?"

"Oh. How'd you find out about that?"

"Your mother left a message on the answering machine. While you were listening to it, I overheard. What's she so happy about? She said she was so happy, remember? Do I have some incurable disease I don't know about?"

"Now, Terry, watch that tongue of yours. My mother happens to like you. It's nothing personal; she just wants the best for me, that's all. And she thinks you and I are too different."

"So should I make dinner for them?" Teresa asked.

"I didn't think you'd want to see them, so I didn't plan anything. Just forget about it."

"Of course I want to see them! This cold war with your family is really getting to me! They pretend I don't exist! It wasn't my fault I was raised in Jersey City!"

"Let's just drop the subject, Terry, mi amor. O.K.?"

"Do I hear conflict?" groaned Obatalá. "Nah! These two have never known how to have a good fight."

"Go back to sleep, Obatalá. We're not there yet. Is that Kentucky Fried Chicken I see?" asked Eleggua. "Hey, Armando, cabrón. It's Kentucky Fried Chicken, stop!"

Again, they drove in silence for a good part of the way. Once in a while Armando would shoot a sideway glance at Teresa and act as if he were ready to say something, but then he'd remain quiet.

"There it is." Teresa broke the silence. "Sagtikos. That should lead us straight to Captree State Park; it's written in green here on the map. I hope it's not a golf course. No, because then there's a little gray road to Robert Moses. Armando, we forgot to buy the shovel!"

"We'll stop somewhere around here."

"Kentucky Fried Chicken!" yelled Eleggua. "Stop! Armando, cabrón! Damn! Missed it again! Goin' to crawl into this dead cat and eat whatever chicken's in there!"

A quarter of an hour later Armando parked the car in front of a hardware store and said he'd be right back.

"We're here!" yelled Shangó.

"Great! Let me go work on the tire," said Obatalá, "I'm gonna slash it."

"And, Armando," Teresa yelled to him. "Maybe you could buy a box? You know, to put him in? We can't just bury him without a little coffin, can we?"

"Ssssh! Terry, mi amor. Someone's going to hear us!"

Soon he was back with a shovel and a box of 24 tall kitchen bags, saying that this was the best he could do. "What do you know, we have a flat tire," he noticed.

✸ ✸ ✸

"Oh. By the way, I'll be in Virginia next weekend. For a golf seminar," Armando said after they'd finally gotten some-one to change the tire and were backing out of the parking space.

"But your parents are coming next weekend!"

"Well, they'll meet me in Virginia. At the golf club. There! See the sign? This should lead us straight there. There sure is a lot of traffic. I thought we'd be all by ourselves, but maybe once we get there. This is probably just local traffic. It can't be people going to the park, can it? So once we get there, I stay in the car, you get off, look for a place, then come back for the shovel. And if anything happens, I'll honk. If you hear me honking, you hide the shovel someplace and come back to the car."

"So you're meeting them in your club in Virginia and leaving me behind."

"I just wanted to spare you the trouble."

"How considerate of you, Armando. So I'm the one who's supposed to dig the grave?"

"Yeah, then I'll go with the cat while you watch the car, and I'll bury him. This'll be all over in no time."

"Boy, what team work!"

When they finally reached Captree State Park, they drove around until they found a place on the side of the road to idle the car. Then they proceeded with the plan. But no sooner had Teresa gotten out of the car and disappeared into the bushes, when a policeman stopped next to their car. "The police is here!" screamed Yemayá. "Run for your lives!"

"It's O.K. They're not illegals. Should we get this cabrón arrested? No way! He has to break the news to her. I'm the one who organized this traffic jam. If not, he'll never tell her. He's a coward. He'll leave her in the dark. At least sixteen more years. Until she's fifty. No! She has to find out."

The officer asked Armando if everything was all right. Armando replied that yes, everything was fine, that it was a beautiful day and that his wife had simply gone into the bushes for a minute, ha ha! Oh, yes, she'd be right back. Oh, yes, absolutely. Armando said that he understood that it was illegal to stop your car anywhere around here, except in designated areas. Of course, he knew all that. Yes, and they weren't supposed to disturb the wildlife or the plants or litter or drink alcoholic beverages. Yes, he understood perfectly. As a matter of fact, Babalú told Armando that he had nothing to feel guilty about since he'd never done any of those things. Never broken the law. He was a perfect citizen. Never littered in a state park. Never thrown litter anywhere at all. Never let a dog off a leash. What he'd done wasn't even prohibited in a state park, imagine that! And state parks sure have a lot of rules. Not illegal anywhere around here. Might as well take this lightly. Who cares about Teresa. She wasn't a broken rule, was she?

It happened three times. Whenever they stopped somewhere to inspect if the ground was fit for burial, a policeman would appear out of nowhere and ask if everything was all right. Maybe Long Island wasn't such a good idea after all. So, they both voted for the Jamaica Bay wildlife refuge in Queens. "If they're going to Queens, I'm staying in Queens," said Obatalá. "Some people are throwing a big party for me there so I'll get them a green card."

Again, Armando opened the map book to page 69. "So, let's take 27 all the way to...oh, 27 turns orange here. In any case, all the way to this blue highway here near Kennedy, then take this orange one. Hold it, page 65. Yeah, the orange one's Cross Bay Boulevard, and we're sure to find a place in Queens. As a matter of fact, we should've gone straight there."

Right when 27 turned orange, Armando finally blurted out, "Terry, mi amor, I have something to tell you. You know how much I love you and how devoted I am to you. But I can't marry you."

"Well, I've known for years that you won't marry me, and now you can't...The terminology seems to have changed."

"O.K., everybody sit back," ordered Shangó. "And I don't want to hear a peep out of anyone!"

"Well," he hesitated. "First I really want you to know how devoted I am to you, but you know I've always had my dreams and ambitions, just like you, which is normal. Don't you think it normal? I mean, for a while I tried to fight it, but my principles seem to be so deeply imbedded in me that surely, but surely, I'm coming to the conclusion that they'll always be there, kind of. Well, not kind of, and the dreams and ambitions, too. I mean, you just can't negate the principles you've been brought up with. Do you follow me?"

"No," replied Teresa.

"O.K., so let's try to reword this. For example, I've never told you this, but my axiom was that the day I'd get engaged—and don't take this personally, Terry, mi amor, it has nothing to do with you, it's a matter of silly deep-rooted principles—anyway, my axiom was that the day I'd get engaged, my future father-in-law would take me to a very exclusive golf club and that we'd spend the day together playing golf and talking business. Now, I've never told you this, but I've told it to other people and they've understood, so please make an effort, Terry, love. Now, you know, José, your father, he's a great guy, you know how much I like him, but he's been working in that laundromat all his life."

"Oh, no, not all his life," said Teresa. "Before that he was a plasterer, but he could paint, too. That was when my mother was a maid. But if you're hung up on fancy clubs, he used to go to one every single day. Ask him if you don't believe me. The toilets there needed cleaning every single day. Sorry to interrupt you, go on."

"Somehow, I knew you wouldn't take this well. But anyway, José, your father, God bless him, for he's a good man, has had this kind of very limited existence. You yourself admit it. You know, for him talking about the economy means comparing Goya beans to Kirby beans and debating whether the frozen tamale or the frozen croquette businesses will thrive. And his world is just so limited to Jersey City. Not that I have anything against Jersey City; you were raised there and look how well you turned out. But do you follow me?"

"Yes, she's beginning to get the drift," said Yemayá.

"I'm staying here in Queens, guys," said Obatalá. "This woman's got no blood in her veins. After what he told her! And she hasn't even cut him!"

"Me, too, I'm getting off," said Ogún.

"This is like the end of a bullfight," snickered Babalú. "And with a very polite bull."

"Cut it out, she's a sweet girl," said Eleggua.

They didn't have any luck at the Jamaica Bay Wildlife Refuge either. So they took the Rockaway Freeway, crossed the Marine Parkway Bridge, and took the Shore Parkway. Armando and Teresa also crossed the Verazano Narrows Bridge, got lost in Staten Island, then wondered if they'd have any luck finding a place to bury the cat in New Jersey. The Bayonne Bridge took them straight into Bayonne and they thought they'd never get out of there. Night fell when they were driving around in North Bergen. There seemed to be no place in the world to bury a fourteen-year-old cat who had fallen out the window that very same morning so long ago when Teresa still thought that she'd spend the rest of her life with Armando.

"Or maybe we should try to bury him in a golf course after all," Teresa said once they had given up and were at the Tappan Zee Bridge toll.

"But that's not all I had to say to you, Terry, mi amor. Something happened last weekend. Or let's say that it happened last weekend. I got engaged, and I went to play golf, with her father. That's the reason my mother called, so happy."

That's when Shangó unsheathed his sword and Yemayá started running all over the world looking for another man for Teresa.

"Chicken wings! That place has take-out chicken wings!" said Eleggua.

It was a little before ten p.m. when they arrived home having found no place to bury the cat.

In the elevator, holding the dead bundle in his arms, Armando shot a sideway glance at Teresa. The beautiful, giggling, party-loving Oshún, who loved Armando's genitals so much, had just reminded him that Teresa would probably find someone else soon. It made Oshún laugh so hard to notice that she'd just put lust and jealousy in his body.

She said, "I am having the time of my life!"

Teresa wiped a tear off her face. Then it was her turn to glance at Armando. She was holding a bucket of extra-spicy chicken wings in her arms. Eleggua was sitting on top of it. He was all excited. "African Powers that surround our Savior," Teresa prayed. "Babalú Ayé, Oshún, Eleggua, Orula, Ogún, Shangó, Yemayá, Obatalá, help me get over this man."

"She summoned me first, did you hear that?!"

LIFE INSURANCE

On the west side of the Hudson River, overshadowed by the New York City skyline, there was a little brick house with a concrete yard. It was three o'clock in the afternoon and Antonio Machado was at home because he had quit his job.

For the past six years he had been working as a Spanish-speaking sales agent in a Fortune 500 life insurance company, Monday through Friday from eight-thirty to six, and performing at the Quetzal Lounge every Friday and Saturday night, so as not to lose touch with his musical side. This is the way he had been inching his way forward through the years. Self-contentedly. Uneventfully. Nothing bad had ever happened to him. Nothing really good either. He had considered himself lucky not to be unlucky and he had been relatively happy, proud of himself, often bragging about how he was a good up-and-coming businessman, a playwright, and an athlete.

Then not so long ago he realized that he was almost thirty-five. "This happens to many people," his mother explained. "But it's no reason to quit your job," she insinuated. "It probably even happens to everyone," she insisted. "Don't you think everyone would prefer to spend their days writing songs and plays?!" she yelled. But Antonio's mind was set.

"It's about time I did something with my life," he said. "My life depends on it," he added.

He felt somewhat disoriented; it had been years since he had been home at this specific time on a weekday. He even wondered, for a minute, if he'd done the right thing. Wasn't it a bit bold? Perhaps this did happen to everyone. But everyone didn't simply quit their job! *No, I did what I had to,* he tried to decide once and for all. *"My life depends on this,"* he kept repeating to himself. He wondered if he should begin right away, waste no time, put his portfolio together, start writing songs and plays. Or just call Sylvia, tell her the news. He had finally taken that courageous leap, he was jobless, and free. So many things to do, but Antonio just sat there, listlessly, far too overwhelmed by the time he had on his hands and the multiple possibilities.

His mother wasn't making this first day any easier. She got herself all worked up in the morning when he told her there was no need to iron his shirt because he wasn't going to work today, nor tomorrow, no he wasn't sick, ahem! as a matter of fact he had no intention of ever returning to the office, why be so surprised? hadn't he told her about it already? Yes, indeed, he had talked about it, she admitted, but an ocean lies between talking and doing. Once again she lectured him on the dangers of quitting your job when everybody else is being laid off. And what about health insurance? He had had such a good policy at the insurance company, it covered dental and all, and if he had to pay it all himself, it would cost around ten-thousand dollars a year, which he couldn't possibly afford with the money he'd be making at the nightclub.

After lunch she stood up, solemnly declared that it was useless to try to make him listen to good reason, and swore that she would never ever utter another single word of advice or disapproval again in her life. But Antonio could still hear her in the kitchen, half-nagging, half-doing the dishes, and at the same time listening to the news on WQBA, a radio station on the am dial that claimed to be the most Cuban, *La Cubanísima.*

Antonio was sitting on the brown and beige living-room couch, legs crossed in a triangle, shaking his left foot as if he were in a dentist's waiting room, and staring at the plastic roses on the coffee table. His mind slowly wandered away from the professional quandaries.

He counted: Sylvia, Elva, Marianita. His mother had chased those three away. They weren't good enough; either too wild, too irresponsible, or too liberated. Then Gloria, Silviana, and Yolanda left him because they definitely could not stand his mother. So he had given up on trying to find the woman of his life and had gone back to picking up girls on street corners and in bars.

"*Vieja!*" he shouted to his mother who was still making kitchen noises. "This couch's way too big for the living room!

It's like a freight train parked in here. Are you listening to me, *Vieja*?"

"No, I'm not listening! And if you hadn't quit your job you wouldn't be here on a Monday, in the middle of the afternoon criticizing the furniture. Tonito, you used to be so busy on Mondays!"

"And these plastic roses are really tacky. Can't you turn that radio down?"

"No, I can't turn it down. The news is bad." The running tap water didn't drown her voice. "Big companies are going out of business, even the banks are in trouble, look at what happened on Wall Street right there across the river and you go and quit your job and decide to become an artist and make your living working full-time in a vulgar drug-and-prostitute infected nightclub on Bergenline Avenue which means that I won't only lose sleep on Fridays and Saturdays waiting up for you like like like I've done for the past five years, oh no your poor old mother had it too easy now you want her to fret and lose sleep five nights a week! I swear, Antonio, the only thing I pray for now is that I die in peace."

"You're talking just like the radio, *Vieja*....Anyway, I've tried, I've tried for years."

"All you've ever tried to do is torment your poor old mother and believe me you've succeeded."

And Antonio wasn't making it any easier on himself either. Sitting there on the living room couch he came to the emotional conclusion that he had lost fifteen years of his life. This got the fretful thoughts going. With stenographic alacrity, his imagination summoned up a list of personal and professional failures. And since the imagination can get so carried away, soon there was a long line of items waiting to be added to the list.

In little or no time, Antonio was already pondering over item number seven: trying to study medicine, because he was in love with Sylvia Bos and dreamt about forming a team. Number eight: business, because his mother told him to. Never did get that MBA, he remembered. Then law, because his mother changed her mind about business. And years ago he had resolved to work out there in the real world—either as a Spanish-speaking life insurance salesman or as an account executive in an Hispanic advertising agency—and struggled to make real money and really tried to encounter what his mother called real people, as opposed to older children. *Not much luck there either*, he thought just before landing on the lowest emotional point which was: *that sums it up, that's my whole existence. Oh, my God!* he panicked. *That's my background! My résumé! My foundation! My person!!"*

Some comforting thoughts came to the rescue. He was an artist, he decided. And a many-sided artist. His skills included guitar playing, singing, and acting. Moreover, he was endowed with a creative mind. He could write plays and compose songs. He just hadn't had time. *Maybe it's not all that bad.* He scratched the back of his neck and wondered if he should give himself a little slack.

✳   ✳   ✳

Antonio's mother quickly blamed Sylvia Bos for her son's reversal. From that day on, the two words "Poor Tonito!" became Nilda's hourly dirge. She told everyone at the laundromat that Antonio had been carefree and self-important up until "Sylvia Bos advised him to throw his hands up in the air, quit selling life insurance, step out of the race, and walk around like a unicorn with the flag of surrender sticking out of his forehead!" She was so worried about him! He didn't even have health insurance anymore! He who used to have full coverage! Dental and all! What if he got sick and needed a doctor?! "Nobody can afford a doctor in this country!" Nilda exclaimed. And she'd never seen poor Tonito this idle and depressed! He spent Tuesday and Wednesday watching soap operas with her. He didn't eat a thing on Thursday! And all day Friday he spent sitting at his desk, trying to write a play. He seemed to hate himself! Especially that he hadn't come up with a single idea or word. So what should she do?! Stand by helpless while this dear child suffered and lost weight?!

Nilda was so worried that she took to eavesdropping whenever Antonio talked to Sylvia Bos on the phone. Antonio complained of being utterly anxious and displeased at the thought of time passing. He feared dying without having accomplished his goals (and this was really absurd, for how could this child that she had brought into the world die?). He even thought he was old! And he was only thirty-five. How could he even think that it might be too late for him to start all over again when his life was just barely beginning?! Was

he going crazy? Of course not! This was definitely Sylvia's
fault.

"My life depends on this," Antonio kept repeating to
Sylvia.

As things stood, while his two younger brothers had been
out there loose and productive in the world for years now,
Antonio hadn't even managed to move out of the maternal
household. And it didn't even seem likely that he'd move out
in any near or distant future, for he was barely starting out,
"all over again for the umpteenth time," he whined to Sylvia.
He also said that his life was a never-ending struggle to
squeeze a penny out of anyone who would have him. He was
ready to go anywhere, to do anything out there in New York
City, and he wondered how he could expect to get anywhere,
much less move out of his mother's house, with this kind of
prideless attitude. And he kept repeating, "My life depends on
this."

A month after having quit his job, he was still distraught,
but he did keep trying to write a play. What kept him going
was the dream that this still unwritten play would be produced on stage. Sylvia continued to encourage him. And one
day after having talked with her for an hour on the phone,
Antonio swore that he would stand firmly by his decision. He
said he had faith in himself. Coincidentally, that was the day
when he finally started to write a play.

* * *

The weeks passed. Antonio kept writing. He considered
himself lucky to be working nights at the Quetzal Lounge. It
allowed him to write and to search for an interesting job during the day. Sylvia, who was his "connection" to the glittering
world outside, was constantly giving him names and
addresses. And once his play was finished, she was the one
who advised him to submit it to El Grupo del teatro panamer-
icano. She thought it was a great play. Antonio followed her
advice, and his imagination did the rest. Since there were so
many dream sequences in this play and it called for so many
strange costumes, he thought they'd need a costume designer!
A big cast! It would run for years. And they would have to
advertise it! In *New York Magazine*!

The people from El Grupo said they'd get back to him. Thirteen weeks later, still no news, and Antonio was in the mire of thinking that it had been too good to be true. There wasn't even anyone to tell him whether the board of directors of El Grupo was considering his play or had burnt it and thrown it in the garbage. He kept begging Sylvia to call them. He said he didn't dare. He wondered if he was jinxed. Did they absolutely loathe and despise his play? Were they repulsed by the playwright, too? Where they telling themselves that he wasn't even worth the phone call?

Every day Nilda asked Antonio if he had heard from El Grupo, and for thirteen whole weeks Antonio made an effort to reply "not yet!" After that, since he was quite an emotional young man, he began to say that each and every one of his fair prospects had gone up in smoke and that he had no choice but to spend his whole life singing at the Quetzal Lounge and that for being such an utter failure, that's what he deserved anyway.

"Antonio! You promised you'd quit working at the nightclub! This is your last month there, isn't it?"

"I said that because I thought my play would be produced on stage," Antonio whined.

"Antonio! The streets in this neighborhood are dangerous! Especially at night! Please! Do it for me! Quit working there! I've had this bad feeling for weeks!"

"And I've studied Karate for years! I'm practically invincible!"

"But I've had this terrible feeling!"

✳ ✳ ✳

That following Friday at eleven a.m., just when Antonio was getting ready to rush off to a casting session, Nilda walked into his bedroom and handed him a large manila envelope that had just arrived in the mail. Antonio shot an aching glance at it and thanked her distractedly.

"It's from El Grupo. Aren't you going to open it?" Nilda asked.

"Probably just a brochure or something," Antonio mumbled while splashing Pierre Cardin after-shave on his face.

"You're not going to wear that shirt, are you?"

"What's wrong with my shirt?" he asked in a hurry while pulling the curtains and letting the September sun shine across the neatly made little bed where he slept. The bed-spread matched the curtains and the cover on his night table, a cream-toned Scottish pattern that his mother had chosen for his chaste male-spinster bedroom.

"That shirt has not been starched. Take it off! I'll go get a fresh one for you! Please open the envelope!"

"*Vieja*, I'm really in a hurry."

"Well, they can wait! I forbid a son of mine to leave this house with a tired-looking shirt! Aren't you going to open the envelope? Don't waste time! If they don't want it, we should send it to someone else today!"

But Antonio refused to open the large manila envelope. He slipped it into his attaché case and impatiently waited for his mother to bring him his shirt. When she finally walked into his bedroom with the impeccable garment on a hanger, he quickly changed, kissed her good-bye, hurried out of the house, and ran up Beach Street toward Palisade Avenue. This seemed to be an important casting from what one of Sylvia's thousand "connections" had said, so Antonio didn't want to miss the gypsy van or get stuck in the midday Lincoln Tunnel traffic.

But apparently Sylvia had gotten it all wrong this time. When Antonio left the Park Avenue South studio, it was already six p.m. He'd wasted a whole day only to hear that they didn't even remotely want his type for this particular tv commercial. *"Sylvia really got this pointer upside-down,"* he said to himself again. A blonde girl with stretch pants sud-denly caught his eye. He stood there and watched her cross the street. "Might as well walk to the Port Authority bus ter-minal," he mumbled, and his mind was already off on another tangent.

It took him around twenty minutes to get to forty-second and eighth. He could catch the six-thirty bus, be home by ten to seven, have a quick dinner, shower, change, rush off to work....It was Friday night; he knew he wouldn't be in bed before five a.m.

It turned out to be a pretty good night after all. He had fun. As usual. In truth, he only hated the Quetzal Lounge when he wasn't there. Or rather, he hated the thought of hav-ing such a loser's job that his mother didn't approve of. But

once he was there it was O.K. He was busy all night, with relatively no time to think about his failed ambition, love problems, fear of dying a bachelor and what not, thus giving his
anxious mind a good deal of rest. Often when he drove home
in the wee hours of the morning, instead of feeling worn he
felt refreshed. Furthermore, it was at the club that he tried
out his own songs. And the public always seemed to appreciate them. At least they momentarily stopped talking and
applauded whenever a song was over. Lately this was his only
source of pride and satisfaction. Not only that, but it also
made him happy, and Antonio had this impatient thirst for
happiness.

Had a lot to drink that night though. And snorted a lot of
coke. He was always trying to steer away from that temptation, but his friend, El Flaco, showed up and said in English
and in Spanish, "What it be, man?! Still busting your ass? Got
something for you, brother, *pa ti toma pa ti mano anda mano!*
A good price!" So Antonio couldn't turn it down and reassured
himself with the thought that this "just once again" wouldn't
necessarily ruin his manhood. But he still remembered it had
been so embarrassing that time with Belkys when he couldn't
come and then it just went limp on him. Now he couldn't even
get around to saying hello to Belkys, who also lived on Beach
Street, three doors away from him. Maybe she'd told the
whole neighborhood that he was impotent or something....
Anyway, he wasn't planning to have a girl that night (which
reminded him that he hadn't had one in about four months
now), so a little coke couldn't hurt. On the contrary, it'd probably do him good, especially since he was so anxious to
remain happy. For the rest of the evening he thought about
meeting the woman of his dreams, a blonde, blue-eyed beauty
called Sandra because he absolutely adored the name Sandra.
And he'd be the only man in her life. And he'd chastely ask
her to marry him. Then he got a hard-on.

Day was breaking when he arrived home, and he still had
a hard-on, partly because of the coke. Right away he was
lucky enough to find a parking space right in front of the
house. "Parking situation's getting worse by the day," he
mumbled to himself. Where to meet that woman? his mind
was always going off on a tangent. Maybe Sylvia could help
him. Introduce him to someone. Have his play put on stage,

fall madly blindly in love, and move out of his mother's. That's all he wanted. *Is that too much to ask?* he wondered.

Every night when he was at the Quetzal Lounge, his mother would light vigil candles to Saint Veronica so he would return home safely. She adamantly refused to go to bed when he wasn't at home, for how would she know if there had been a fire at the club or if he had had a car accident? So she preferred to wait up for him half-asleep half-awake sitting on the living room couch in front of the television set. If anything terrible happened she thought she'd get the news right away and could rush off to rescue him. She didn't need much sleep anyway, not even during the week. Three or four hours were enough, and she'd spend the remaining part of her day at the laundromat gossiping, or cooking, dusting, vacuuming, ironing, doing the dishes, cleaning the oven, making sure her son had his three meals, praying, worrying about him, meditating, yelling at him, cajoling him, watching Spanish movies, Spanish soap operas, reading Spanish novels, magazines, or anything that was written in Spanish. After having lived in this country for thirty-two years, her only English words were still "yes," "no," and "hello," and two or three other elementary words she had brought with her from Cuba. These thirty-two years hadn't so much as touched her; she had remained totally impervious to the language, the country, the culture, except that she repeated, "This is the best country in the world!" along with all the other Cubans in the neighborhood. "No fear of Communism!" But to her a quarter remained *"un cora,"* and a dollar *"un peso."* She didn't need English anyway, not in this neighborhood of Jersey City where they had lived ever since they had arrived in the United States from Cuba.

Then a family of four, they had rented the basement of this very same brick house. Two years later, upon the arrival of a new baby, they rented the first floor and waited another ten years before they bought the whole house. Soon after, Nilda's husband ran off to Miami with another woman, leaving her with three boys to raise, a factory job, and little money. Thanks to the intelligent advice of Delfina Bos, an old friend of hers, Nilda had managed the money well, put her sons through college, did everything to give them their wings. The second boy moved to Texas, the youngest to California, while Antonio, the eldest, whose well-being she had never stopped fretting about, stayed on Beach Street where his

neatly ironed and lightly starched shirts, as well as his three
meals, were always waiting for him.

That Saturday morning, just like every Saturday morning, Nilda opened the front door before Antonio put his key in
the lock. She immediately asked him if he wanted something
to eat. He said no, thank you, he was exhausted and was
dying to go straight to bed.

At one in the afternoon his mother woke him with an
eight-ounce tumbler of carrot juice and a Spanish omelette.
Not quite awake, Antonio told her to put the lunch on his
desk. She did as he asked, then discreetly walked out of the
bedroom.

Wearily, Antonio got out of bed, opened one of his bureau
drawers and searched for some pajama pants to put over his
underwear since his mother would be back in his bedroom in
less than quarter of an hour to make the bed. He then realized he also needed a bathrobe, for he still had that hard-on.
"Where is that bathrobe?" he wondered out loud in a hurry to
find it. From the hallway Nilda yelled, "It's in the bathroom!"

After sitting down to eat, he distractedly put one hand in
his attaché case in the hope of finding something to read
while eating. Just as distractedly, his hand chanced upon the
manila envelope he had received from El Grupo the day
before.

Ten minutes later, Nilda stopped breathing for thirty sec-
onds and put her hand on the telephone receiver in the
kitchen. She had this sixth sense where her Tonio was concerned, and this sixth sense was now telling her that he was
talking to Sylvia. She exhaled, then took in a deep breath and
slowly picked up the receiver.

She loved her son. She adored him. And she had spent all
these years catering to his every need and demand. She'd
hurry out under the rain to buy chicken if at the last minute
chicken was what he wanted to eat. She kept track of his
after-shave lotions and toiletries and was sure to have a
fresh supply in stock before he ran out of anything. She tried
not to meddle in his love life. It was obvious that he had
lovers. While tidying up the mess that he always left on his
bureau, her cleaning hand would inevitably chance upon
some motel bills. Furthermore, he usually kept a box of con-
doms hidden underneath his sunglass cases. She did stealth-
ily keep tab, but it didn't matter that he had them because it

was normal. She even tried to let him make his own professional decisions. O.K., Nilda admitted that she had been a bit
hard on him when he decided to quit his job at the life insurance agency. But now this! She was so upset that she could
only hear bits and pieces of the conversation he was having
with Sylvia. "I've never been as unhappy and as lonely in my
life!" he complained.

"Are you just going to throw your hands up in the air
after one rejection?" Sylvia insisted.

Antonio kept repeating "Monday. First thing in the
morning."

He was going to call his life insurance company and beg
them to take him back! And he swore that he'd never have
any kind of artistic ambition again for as long as he lived.
He'd even quit working at the Quetzal Lounge. Tonight would
be his last night. Just so he could say good-bye to all his buddies there. "This whole experience has been way too painful
for me, Sylvia," he repeated.

Slowly, Sylvia started giving up on him. "I guess you
tried," she said. "Look!" she added. "It's an experience! Now
you can go back to selling life insurance and your heart and
your mind will be at rest because you know that that's what
you want to do! Now you know that you're not really made to
do anything else!"

"No, Sylvia," he replied. "My heart and my mind will
never be at rest again."

After they hung up, Nilda told herself that she should be
happy and relieved. He'd go back to his company, he'd have
health coverage, he'd stop working at the nightclub, he'd be
safe! So why, she wondered, why this sadness? As if someone
had died! She sat at the kitchen table, put her head in her
hands, and cried.

* * *

An hour later, Nilda was running down Beach Street
yelling, "Antonio! Antonio!" She reached him when he was
about to get into his car

"What is it, *Vieja*?" he asked.

"I forgot to tell you," she gasped for air. "I think *Next
Christmas in Havana* is a great play and I'm proud of you for
having written it!"

He thanked her but said it was no use, his mind was made up, he'd quit all that silly nonsense, and he was in a hurry. He had to get to the nightclub and say good-bye to all that forever.

"Take care of yourself," Nilda said.

"Hey, *Vieja*, I've studied Karate for years! Besides, I know the neighborhood. And you should be happy. This is my last night! Why are you so puffy-eyed?"

∗ ∗ ∗

He walked out the nightclub at three a.m. His car was parked several blocks away, on the avenue. When Antonio reached New York Avenue, he heard the smashing of car windows. Another one of those teen-age gangs was having a Saturday night bash. Slowly, noisily, they advanced. The leader was yelling strange commands. It sounded like *ho! yo! wo!*, like war cries. It was a language Antonio could not understand. They resembled a pack of wild animals, except that wild animals, no matter how fierce and hungry, didn't seem to have this raw violence. And they kept smashing car windows. And the leader kept yelling these commands that Antonio could not understand. They advanced like a pack of wild animals. Hyenas? Jackals? Lions? Locust? *Hey, man,* Antonio said to himself, *these are human beings. Don't you go comparing them to a pack of wild animals. Wow! What was that sound? A muffler?* If he was in Union City, New Jersey, why couldn't he understand their language? *There it goes again! Wow! How loud!* And what was this warm liquid next to his cheek? And why were they walking on him? Maybe he should keep on trying. *No, I'm not going back to the insurance company,* Antonio decided. *I'm going to keep on trying. I'm going to keep on writing. Keep on writing.* One bullet through his head, another through his heart. He didn't know he died. On the sidewalk. Before the ambulance arrived.

WHAT MIRANDA LOST

It was early December and a bitter cold day. The atmosphere was crackling with static electricity. Such frigid temperatures were unusual for this time of the year. Miranda Xuárez walked out of the discount pharmacy and held the door open for her sister, Jacobina Flecha. It was Wednesday, in the afternoon, and the sidewalks of downtown Elizabeth, New Jersey, were empty. Both sisters had on several layers of itchy woolens beneath their sad gray-black coats, and their scarves were of the same color. Briskly, they walked toward the bus stop. The metallic wind squeezed their lungs and pulled their ears. They quickened their pace. But suddenly Miranda had to stop, just to make sure, feel around under her scarf. It was so desperately cold that for a minute she thought her nose had fallen off. She even said to Jacobina, "Hold it! I think I lost my nose! Jacobina, it fell off!"

"What a stupid thing to say, Miranda! People don't just lose their nose!"

"I can't feel it, Jacobina!"

"Just because you can't feel it doesn't mean it's not there. Come on! It's too cold to be standing out here on the sidewalk!"

They began walking again. Miranda could barely keep up with her sister. After her nose, she thought she'd lost a toe. "I've never been as cold in my life!" she complained with numb lips that could barely speak. "Where's my ear?!" she then asked fretfully. "Can't wait till I get to Miami, I swear!"

"Keep your mouth shut or you'll catch pneumonia," Jacobina warned her. "And we're almost there. Hurry!"

"I'm hurrying, Jacobina. But I can't feel my toes. How am I going to wear sandals in Miami if I lose my toes? Can't wait till I get to Miami. Can't wait till I..."

"We're here!"

"Now what?" Miranda asked.

They waited and shivered for nearly five minutes. "Saint Anthony, please!" Miranda turned to the industrially blackened old Dutch church and yelled, as if she were angry at the saint. "That's not a Catholic church," Jacobina declared. "Besides, Saint Anthony isn't the one responsible for the weather here."

"It's Fidel! We wouldn't be going through this if Fidel hadn't taken over Cuba!" Miranda complained. "The day I leave for Miami, I'll throw my coat in the garbage," she added, just to feel better, and warmer.

Still no sign of the bus though. Miranda walked to the middle of the street and looked. No bus. What should they do? Wait a little longer? Freeze here? What about a little cup of coffee? In that cafeteria. They both pointed to the cafeteria ten steps away and briskly walked toward it, pushed the glass door open, two sisters talking at the same time, Miranda saying that Saint Anthony had given them this good idea, Jacobina saying that apparently, from what she'd heard, even the weather in Cuba had made a turn for the worse since Fidel. Never been as many hurricanes!

"A fine day you pick to buy hair spray!" Jacobina said, once they were seated at the counter. She hadn't even taken her gloves off. They decided to order two *cafecitos* and pay right away and run out of there the minute they saw the bus. For once they agreed, they were both dying to be home.

"Oh! My hair!" Miranda whined as she pulled off her scarf. "I hate this static!"

Several strands of Miranda's hair were sticking up on top of her head. They had finally let go of the scarf and were reaching for the ceiling now. She put her hand up there and could feel each electrified strand. Her hand was like a magnet. Then someone passed behind Miranda on his way to the cashier and her hair made a crackling leap for his coat. So much for Miranda's Jacqueline Kennedy hairdo! It was gone. Jacobina said there was nothing but an electrocuted bird's nest up there now. At least Miranda had the hair spray. She'd work on her hair when she got home. She couldn't live without hair spray. Hair spray was what made her look like Jacqueline Kennedy, and more than anything in the world Miranda wanted to look like Jacqueline Kennedy and lead the same kind of life. And perhaps she wasn't quite as thin as Jacqueline, but she had the same brown hair and she had named her twins John and Jacqueline. They had been born during what Miranda considered to be the Kennedy reign. And in her heart, the Kennedys still reigned even if John Kennedy had been assassinated and replaced by Lyndon Johnson and Jacqueline was no longer the first lady.

Miranda loved repeating her children's first names, "John! Jacqueline!" Her elder daughter, on the contrary, had been born too early, in Cuba, in 1960, a few months before Kennedy was elected president, and even before Miranda had heard about the Kennedys. So her name was Enriqueta, Kiki for short. She had been named after one of the Xuárez's ancestors who had supposedly given Hernán Cortés a child back in the beginning of the sixteenth century. And Miranda still regretted having named her daughter Enriqueta. She would have named her Rose if she had known better. And it was just a matter of months, because shortly after Kiki's birth, Castro declared that he was a Marxist-Leninist and the Xuárez family had to pick up and go after having gotten their smallpox shots. And most important of all, Miranda discovered the Kennedys and fell in love with everything about them, from their wealth to their good looks to their lifestyle.

Alas, Miranda's husband, Tomás Xuárez, was only a Math teacher, "and you can't get very far on a teacher's paycheck," Miranda always nagged. "But at least your children will have a good education," her sister Jacobina argued.

Jacobina was a widow and had but one child, a twelve-year-old named Carlos. And Jacobina wasn't ambitious in the same way as Miranda. Jacobina was a dressmaker who worked twelve hours a day, then ran to the bank and put the hard-earned money in savings so her son could go to the best university one day and become a professional.

Miranda was always criticizing Jacobina's slow principle of effort. "Why literally work your fingers to the bone?" she asked her sister. "You've only got one life!" she'd warn Jacobina. And it was no use "waiting." Had to take what you could. Try to make it the best possible life. It was the only one. That's why Miranda wanted her husband to quit teaching Math and start a business, something like general contracting, which was, supposedly, where the money was. "Everybody has to live somewhere! Am I wrong or am I right?" Miranda repeated. So general contracting was necessarily the business to be in. Either that or food, because "Everybody has to eat! Am I wrong or am I right?"

"How in the world do you expect a Math teacher to become a general contractor?" Jacobina asked Miranda.

"Others have made it!" Miranda would answer with a wave of the hand that signified her impatience. "Others have succeeded. Why not us? I want the best for my family!"

For the past five years Miranda and Jacobina had been sharing the same house in Elizabeth. Jacobina had the first floor with Carlos, her son, and the Xuárez family had the spacious, sunny second floor. They rented the basement to an elderly couple.

Tomás had decreed—and this is the only thing he had ever decreed, for he was a gentle man who dearly loved and obeyed his wife—Tomás had decreed that the general well-being of the family was of utmost importance. It came before everything, even before each individual's personal satisfaction. So each adult member of the family was given a particular task or responsibility with this goal in mind—the well-being of the family. Tomás was the main provider, he taught Math and Latin. Jacobina supplied an additional income, she made dresses for a living. And, Tomás and Jacobina both being so busy, Miranda was put in charge of the housework and of the children. This should have worked out and made existence smooth and easy, except that whatever Miranda did, she did unwillingly. She spent her life nagging and complaining. Every single night she quarreled with Tomás. She hated getting up in the morning to make breakfast for the children. Jacqueline Kennedy probably never had to do that. So why didn't she, Miranda Xuárez, have a half-decent existence? Didn't she deserve it? Why did Jacqueline Kennedy have something she couldn't have? Then the school bus honked. Then she had to clean up after the children. Would it be this way forever? Was this all she was going to get? Was it her fate to spend the rest of her days doing housework in a tacky little house in Elizabeth? Why was everyone luckier than she? It was when she was bewildered by moods such as these that she quarreled the most with her husband, children, sister, and nephew. "Am I supposed to do the housework while you're lazily twiddling your thumbs at school with your feet up on your desk?" she'd call Tomás at school and ask. This is how she imagined that his days at school went.

She was convinced that teaching was a lazy man's career and always imagined Tomás giving the children tests and spending the day either twiddling his thumbs, or reading, or both. When he brought home papers to correct, she'd also go into fits of rage. Why was he bringing work home when he'd done absolutely nothing all day? If he spent a little less time doing less than nothing all day, he probably wouldn't have to bring work home and ruin everyone's evening.

"And am I supposed to do the dishes while you spend the day gossiping with your clients?" she'd angrily ask her sister. Miranda was convinced she had gotten the worst deal possible, the worst half of everything. And why was that? Because she was too good. Because she was gullible and let everyone take advantage of her and always put everybody else's well-being before her own. Because Tomás had practically ordered, yes, ordered her to give up her own personal satisfactions. But she was going to stop having such a generous heart. She was going to start thinking about herself at least a little more. She swore on her Saint Anthony medal and crossed her heart. Because everyone had it better, everyone was taking advantage of her. Even the children had it too good. They were either at school doing nothing, or playing ball, or playing out in the street while she was either folding laundry or vacuuming. She shed tears and repeated that she was a good woman, as good as they come, so she didn't deserve such bad luck.

Miranda hated everything about her life. She hated everything that surrounded her. She hated the house, the street, the people, what she considered to be her sister's lack of ambition, her husband's laziness, the children's attitude. Every single mother in the world was luckier than she, starting with Jacqueline Kennedy. She also hated the town, the weather, the whole state of New Jersey...Ever since they had arrived in New Jersey from Cuba, Miranda's sole aim had been to get out of New Jersey. For years she had dreamt of Miami and had even bought maps of that city so she could imagine herself walking down certain seaside avenues. She spent hours with the map unfolded in front of her on the kitchen table. She wondered on what street she would live once she got there. Life seemed so easy in Miami! All she had to do was pick a street, imagine a house, a lawn, a driveway, a Cadillac!

Maybe Tomás would quit being a Math teacher and start
a general-contracting business once they moved to Miami. Oh,
everything would be so much better in Miami! And whether
that "lazy bum" she had married would change careers or not,
Miami was the place where she would surely be happy. Not
only was the weather in Miami spectacular, but from what
she'd heard it even resembled Cuba! Cuba before Castro. So
maybe life there would turn out to be just the way it had been
in Cuba. Miranda liked to reminisce out loud in front of her
sister who couldn't believe her ears because Miranda would
get so carried away that she invented herself a past that
never really existed. She talked about the fortune she'd left
behind in Cuba. "What fortune?" Jacobina would ask.
Miranda would never answer, she'd just continue reminiscing.
The house, the money, the servants, the jewelry, the horses,
the silver! A Jacqueline Kennedy life! Miranda often wept
because she had supposedly lost all that. This was her way of
accepting Jacqueline Kennedy's wealth and good looks. The
former first lady had turned into Miranda's Mrs. Jones. So in
order to keep herself from dying of envy, Miranda began seeing in Jacqueline Kennedy the paradise she had lost. Perhaps
she was poor and led a mediocre life now, but she'd left a fortune behind in Cuba. Miranda wouldn't have it any other
way. It was no use trying to convince her that the past had
not been that perfect. They had been rich in Cuba. Extremely
so.

"We weren't rich!" Jacobina would argue.

"Oh, yes we were!" Miranda retorted. "We were born with
golden spoons in our mouths!"

"And nothing to eat!" Jacobina laughed.

"You just don't want to remember, Jacobina."

And if Jacobina didn't want to remember, it was because
she had no ambition. She preferred to forget and accept life as
it was and allow herself to become a common, mediocre person. That wasn't for Miranda though. Every Friday afternoon
when she pulled a raw chicken out of the refrigerator,
Miranda swore that she'd die rather than become part of
what she called the "common denominator." For some reason,
this mathematical term evoked the image of a swarming
crowd of people who would never succeed in life. Miranda
would angrily cut the chicken up, chop the garlic in a mortar,
and chant to herself that she would certainly never become

part of the common denominator. While the chicken's watery blood dripped in the kitchen sink, Miranda thought that the common denominator was probably something that mathematicians avoided. Perhaps that was the whole point of mathematics, staying clear of the common denominator. She'd have to ask "that lazy bum" Tomás.

"It would be so different in Miami," she dreamt and pounded and pounded on the garlic.

"It'll be so different in Miami!" she told her sister Jacobina while they were sitting in that cafeteria waiting for the bus on that metallic Wednesday. All the rich Cubans were in Miami. Money practically grew on Florida soil. Miranda opened a parenthesis to mention that tragedy often struck the jet-set Cuban families: cancer, car accidents, adultery, murder, divorce, heart attacks. The rich suffer, too. Miranda was well aware of it, and she just couldn't stop turning the cliché over in her mouth, relishing it, like the hot cafeteria coffee on such a cold day, one comment leading to another, the topic seemed inexhaustible. So and so was so rich and died of a heart attack at forty-eight. What a pity. Wonder where his millions went? Poor widow. "But it's better to cry for a rich husband than for a poor husband," Miranda said.

"God should punish you for saying such terrible things!" Jacobina yelled. "I hope He does. I really do. You don't even know what you're talking about!"

"He's punished me enough already. O.K., Jacobina, don't get mad. I'm sorry I said that. It's because I'm so unhappy. Let's change the subject, O.K.? It'll be so different in Miami. I'm so excited!"

It so happened that Tomás had been offered a teaching position in a Catholic girls' school in Miami for September of that following year. The news had arrived the week before, and Miranda had been gleaming with enthusiasm ever since. "It'll be so different in Miami!" she kept repeating. "We'll become rich!"

"Tomás is still going to be a teacher," Jacobina mentioned. "So I don't see why you'd become rich," she said casually.

"But I'll convince him! I'll make him take evening classes. I'll tell him that he's been on vacation all his life and that it's about time he began real life and that he has to think about his children and this'll make him feel guilty, so in a year or so he'll be a general contractor. That's where the money is! Not only that, Jacobina, but he's going to teach at the Academy of the Assumption, and you probably don't know it, but that's where all the daughters of the rich families go, families that are extremely rich and who weren't like us who left all our fortune in Cuba. They had their money in bank accounts right here, or in Switzerland."

"So, do you expect them to give Tomás bonuses after each class?" Jacobina asked, still angry at her sister.

"Private lessons, Jacobina! What do girls have the most difficulty with? Math and Latin. What do girls always need private lessons in? Math and Latin. And what is Tomás going to teach at the Academy of the Assumption? Math and Latin! Don't you get it, Jacobina?! However it turns out to be, we'll be rich! And if you don't believe me, let's compare our lives in let's say twenty years. Let's see where you'll be and where I'll be! Let's see where our children will be! Carlos will be thirty-two...Kiki twenty-seven...John and Jacqueline will be...

It was such a cold day in Elizabeth, New Jersey. Miranda and Jacobina were sitting in a cafeteria next to the old Dutch church waiting for a bus to take them home. Miranda just couldn't wait to get to Miami. "I just can't wait until I'm rich and happy!" she told her sister. "And it should be easy," she added, "because I'll do anything to get what I want." She thought she had nothing to lose. The bus had been rerouted that day. They waited twenty-two years.

✳ ✳ ✳

The day Miranda boarded the plane that was to take her to Miami, she swore she'd never return to New Jersey again. She said something that resembled "fountain, I will not drink your water" and left. Jacobina could always come and visit her.

She chose to live in Miami Beach, where she imagined the rich people to be. And at first it was perfect, especially it was different from Elizabeth, New Jersey. The air was salty and smelled sweet, and the streets and the sidewalks and the houses and the buildings were clean. The Xuárez family moved into a white and blue apartment house on Royal Palm Avenue, a block away from North Beach Elementary School and right across the street from a large food store called

Pantry Pride. Everything was convenient. John could walk to school every day and mingle with rich Miami Beach kids. His sisters were getting free private education at the Academy of the Assumption. As for Miranda, all she had to do was cross the street and there she was in the air-conditioned supermarket, prodding the chicken, sniffing the cantaloupes, touching the pineapples, pushing an icy shopping cart through one of the eight aisles. For the moment the Xuárez family didn't even need two cars.

The building where they lived wasn't too bad either, at least not from the outside; it had this pleasant art-deco squareness to it, huge windows that opened all the way out, and quite a heraldic name: the Royal Arms. And it was quiet, full of elderly couples with Eastern European accents. But it wasn't like Miranda to remain happy. Suddenly she remembered that she had been born with a golden spoon in her mouth and yelled "look at me now! Cooking! Cleaning! Ironing!" She began spending her days in the kitchen, crying and chopping onions and garlic. Sometimes she got so carried away and chopped so many onions that she had to throw them out. And it was so hot in Miami! Couldn't even breathe! Miranda would have fits of rage all by herself. Sometimes she'd take it out on the paper towel, throw it across the kitchen, run to kick it, then throw it out the window. "It stinks in here!" she hissed. Indeed it did. The apartment had this horrible smell that wouldn't go away. Miranda said she ruined her hands with all the detergents she had tried, but the stench remained. It was all over the building, even out in the porch. It got stronger when you opened the rusty, whining, whimpering screen door with that rusty ugly metal flamingo that was bent in two and half-broken and falling off and would one day hurt someone. That horrible door! Couldn't the landlord do something about it? It opened to a dim corridor that also smelled. Miranda began hating the smell of this building about as much as she hated the tawdry imitation-candlestick lamps nailed to the corridor walls. She said it smelled of corpses, mildew, insect repellent, and rotting wet clothes. She complained and cried and shouted. Now, it was every morning and every night that she quarreled with Tomás. The neighbors would knock on their door, bang on their walls, and sometimes even call the police when Miranda, who didn't heed their irate protests, continued screaming at the top of her lungs and throwing anything she could get her hands on at Tomás, even dinner. She said she was born with a golden spoon in her mouth and look at her now, chopping onions and garlic. Smell her hands! They smelled of onion and garlic. "Smell my hair!" she'd say and dishevel her Jacqueline Kennedy hairdo. It smelled like the building! Now look at Jacqueline Kennedy! She'd never done anything demeaning in her life! So why didn't Tomás quit his silly job and study to be a general contractor?!

Tomás was a gentle man. He deeply loved his children and his wife. Miranda's constant nagging hadn't so much as altered the tender feelings he'd had for her since the day they were married. He didn't even mind the nagging. He just thought it necessarily came with a wife. Nagging was probably normal. Women were like that. It had something to do with their cycle. Tomás would have sworn that every single man was henpecked. It was completely normal. He didn't mind this at all. He knew that the minute he walked in the door after a difficult day at the Academy of the Assumption, the first thing he'd hear would be "you no good lazy bum!" followed by "If you were a man, you'd become a general contractor!" But even the nuns at the Academy of the Assumption nagged. It came with being a woman. So why not his wife? Besides, Miranda had been sweet and loving up until the day she found out about Jacqueline Kennedy, so maybe this was just a crisis, maybe it would pass.

What really worried him was those times when Miranda got carried away and yelled that Kiki, John, and Jacqueline would get nowhere in life. Nowhere! And why?! Because of the lazy no-good bum they had for a father. Because their lazy father just refused to budge and make money like all the other fathers! Now look at John Kennedy! He even died so his family could live well! But not Tomás! He was content just being part of the common denominator! But he'd see, one of these days, the boomerang! Before he knew it, Miranda warned, his daughters would have to quit school in order to make a living and probably even have to walk the streets because they were so poor and couldn't make ends meet!

"My love, we're not that poor," Tomás dared to say shyly.

This only made Miranda angrier. Of course they were poor! Dirt poor! If Tomás didn't notice it, that was his problem. He was too busy thinking only of himself, too content with the status quo. But she, Miranda, who was born with a golden spoon in her mouth, couldn't stand it!

Tomás respected his wife's opinion. Once again, he loved her dearly and adored his children. Could it be that his children's lives would be ruined because of him? Was he really a lazy father? By being a modest high-school teacher, was he keeping them from having what all the other children in the world had? But he knew he couldn't become a general contractor. It just wasn't him! He was a math teacher. So he'd have to work with what he had.

During the first two years he spent teaching at the Academy of the Assumption, Tomás refused to give private lessons, convinced as he was that he could easily support his family with his salary. Not only that, but he also wanted to spend time with his wife and children. He liked taking Kiki, John, and Jacqueline to the zoo and the Parrot Jungle. He also enjoyed Sunday afternoon picnics by the lighthouse on Key Biscayne. It was sweet. It made him believe life was sweet. They swam and they had fun, played in the sand and ate hot dogs and cotton candy. Of course Miranda never went with them; the Key Biscayne lighthouse was one of the favorite spots of the "common denominator" which she so feared and hated.

In spite of the loving care and attention Tomás gave Kiki, John, and Jacqueline, Miranda did manage to convince him that he was a bad father. "Those children need money, not attention!" Miranda explained to him whenever she was mellow. What good was a Sunday picnic at the Key Biscayne lighthouse when you're dirt poor and in danger of becoming part of the "common denominator?" So Tomás decided to start giving private lessons, just in case Miranda was right. First it was twice a week, then three times, then every evening. By February of that school year he was even working on the weekends. The year after that he organized group lessons and charged each child ten dollars an hour. When Kiki needed a new outfit, he gave three extra hours of Latin because Miranda wanted her to have the most expensive outfits. Every week he was putting money in the bank in order to surprise Miranda one of these days with a down payment on a house. That's what she needed. Her own house. If she nagged, it was because she was insecure. And that was his fault. He hated himself for that. Miranda wanted to live in Bal Harbour and swore on her Saint Anthony medal that she'd only be happy the day they had their own house. But it had to be a big house, a beautiful house, not one of those "common denominator" houses. Tomás saved money for three long years. He hardly ever got to see his family, but it was for a good reason, to offer them the security they so desperately needed, to prove that he loved them and was a good husband and father. Then Miranda said she absolutely needed the car because she felt trapped all day at the Royal Arms. Tomás understood. He didn't really need a car anyway, it was just parked at school all day. He could take the bus to work. And almost all his students lived near the Academy of the Assumption; he could walk to his private lessons; it would do him good to get a little exercise anyway. And he didn't mind taking the bus to return home. It gave him time to read the paper. As a matter of fact, he told Miranda that this arrangement suited him much better.

The years passed. They finally bought a house in Bal Harbour. The Xuárez children were well-dressed and had everything they wanted. When Kiki turned sixteen, she immediately got a car. Miranda explained that every sixteen-year-old in the world had a car, and she didn't want Kiki to feel inferior to anyone. Then it was John and Jacqueline's turn to turn sixteen. They also got cars, except that John got the nicest one, a beautiful expensive sports car, for John was Miranda's dream come true. Ever since he was eight years old, John had decided that he'd be a general contractor when he grew up. So the Xuárez family became a four-car family. The only member of the family without a car was Tomás.

At least Kiki volunteered to drive him to the Academy of the Assumption every morning. But he didn't want to bother her after school. Anyway, he had at least three private lessons in three different places, and he could either walk or take the bus. He'd get home at ten p.m., and Miranda would accuse him of all sorts of things. They'd quarrel and he'd go to bed without dinner. Miranda said he didn't deserve dinner, that she wasn't his slave! So Tomás' diet consisted of coffee and cigarettes. It didn't really bother him; he loved coffee and cigarettes. The important thing was that he was giving private lessons and that once in a while Miranda assured him that he was a good man and that she appreciated what he was doing. "I guess you're doing the best you can!" she would admit those rare times when she was mellow. Then she would sigh. He really wanted to do his best and make her happy and content.

She fell in love with a bigger house in Bal Harbour. It was expensive and the mortgage was high, but Tomás said, "Let's put the for-sale sign out. If we sell this one for a good price...The mortgage on the other one's a little high. But I can give more private lessons. Don't cry, Miranda, I'll manage."

He did. And the new house was beautiful. It overlooked Biscayne Bay and had an enormous yard and a fountain in the middle of the driveway. Miranda chose a brick-colored roughcast paint for the outside so it would resemble the Hernández-Betancourt house on Star Island. She then had all the bathrooms redone in black marble, had a sunken bathtub installed, and bought a water bed for John with a fur bed-spread, satin sheets for herself, and a cashmere blanket that filled her with longing. "Too bad I have to sleep with Tomás," she thought. "Too bad!" After that, she ordered fancy, curly, Alhambra-like bars for all the windows. That very same day, she rented a cabana at the Fountainbleu Hotel and made an appointment for Tomás to take tennis lessons. She bought all the Louis Vuitton collection, from the key chain to the lug-gage and the shopping bag. John got a Porsche the day he took his SAT exams. Tomás didn't understand why Miranda was so intent on making him take tennis lessons. Miranda explained that the Hernández-Betancourts from Star Island played tennis at the Fountainbleu and the Hernández-Betan-courts were very good connections.

John didn't want to go to college. He wanted to be the president of his own company, and Miranda thought that was fine. He never really learned how to drive a stick shift and blamed it on the bad quality of European cars. He got a huge American car for his eighteenth birthday. When Kiki went away to college, she gave Jacqueline her car. Jacqueline's old car was then traded in for a Gucci Volvo for Miranda. And while Miranda wondered if green was a good color for a Gucci Volvo, Tomás was taking the bus to his Saturday afternoon tennis lesson at the Fountainbleu. He had several private lessons on Saturday morning, but Miranda couldn't lend him her car. Although she didn't swim, or sunbathe, or play ten-nis, she liked getting to the Fountainbleu early on Saturday morning, in her car, just so she wouldn't feel trapped.

One very hot Saturday in the middle of summer, Miranda forced Tomás to take a tennis lesson and nagged about him not being athletic. An hour later he returned to the cabana drenched in sweat, and Miranda made fun of his red face. She even told him he was ugly, then ordered him to go refresh himself in the pool, maybe he'd look less ugly. But Tomás didn't want to go by himself; he said he didn't feel well. So Miranda unwillingly left the shady shelter of her cabana in order to accompany Tomás.

While they were slowly walking on the red deck, he suddenly wanted to hold her hand. She got angry. "Who do you think you are?!" she asked him.

"I just wanted to hold your hand," Tomás protested.

The pool was glittering. Tomás said it looked pretty. Didn't it look pretty? Like a bed of diamonds. "Give me a kiss," Tomás said. "A little kiss, please?"

Miranda then told him he smelled like an old man and pushed him away. She quickly changed the subject. She'd only put her feet in the pool because chlorine does horrors to a woman's skin. She was sitting on the edge making waves, watching Tomás gently splash about in the shallow end, wondering why in the world she'd chosen such an ugly man for a husband. Suddenly Tomás stopped and carefully walked up the underwater stairs and slowly emerged from the pool.

"Tomás, what's the matter?" Miranda asked, still a bit irritated by his looks and his vulnerable presence.

His old brown bathing suit clung to his thin body. He left wet footmarks on the red deck. "What's the matter, Tomás? Don't get sick on me now; we have the worst of insurance policies!" He let himself fall on a lounge chair. He was dead.

Miranda went hysterical. The lifeguard called the paramedics. But there was no heart to pump. It had literally exploded. Miranda couldn't understand what they were saying. The widows in bathing suits with baggy thighs tried to comfort her. They told her that widowhood was painful, but that she'd get over it. After all, what's his name had lived a good life.

"No speek Inglich!" Miranda yelled. "Tomás! Tomás! I want him to come back! Oh my God I killed Tomás!"

✳ ✳ ✳

There are two cemeteries on eighth street; the green grassy one with the expensive plots, and the less grassy one, farther away, for those who can't pay as much. Miranda chose the second one, convinced that poor Tomás would be much happier there.

Two months after the funeral, she had the inside of her house redone because the old furniture reminded her way too much of her late husband, God bless him, such a good caring husband and father who had left his family a quarter of a million dollar insurance policy. Miranda hadn't even known about it. Tomás had gotten this insurance policy in secret, probably knowing that Miranda would have made him give it up if she had ever found out about it. She then traded the old furniture with her maid for a year's work without pay.

After Christmas, Miranda had her stomach redone by a plastic surgeon, then her breasts, then her eyes, then her whole face. She hardly thought of Jacqueline Kennedy anymore, but still wanted to look good so her son would be proud of her and because she was going into the general-contracting business with John, her only "reason for living now that Tomás was gone."

"The boy has a head on his shoulders," she told Jacobina, who came to visit once a year and bored Miranda to tears with her eternal bragging about Carlos who would soon be an engineer.

It was September, right after Labor day when Miami is getting ready for winter and all you see in the Bal Harbour Shops are turtlenecks and mink coats. Miranda was browsing around Neiman Marcus; she had an hour to kill and a three-o'clock appointment at the hairdresser's. She opened her Louis Vuitton credit-card wallet.

"That'll be $507.57," the salesgirl said.

Miranda took the gold credit card out carefully for fear that it might break her nail.

"Isn't that a bit expensive?" Jacobina asked.

"We're going into the general-contracting business," Miranda replied. "Nothing's expensive now. Everybody had to live somewhere. Am I wrong or am I right?"

She had just gotten the "living-cells" line of beauty products created in Austria by a doctor and made of mountain water and minerals that did wonders for your skin overnight.

It was quite warm outside, especially in contrast with the air-conditioned store. Miranda and Jacobina slowly walked down the promenade toward the beauty parlor. The September sun was shining on the little round tables of the European-imitation coffee shops and on the aquamarine-tiled water fountains that produced the soft gentle sounds of water all through the Bal Harbour Mall.

Inside the beauty parlor it smelled of bleach and crimson nail polish. Those smiling ladies, many of them widows like herself, "Miranda Xuárez," she said to the receptionist, "tree o'clo." They gave her a sky-blue robe and told her to sit in the waiting area where five other ladies with sun-streaked hair and Miami tans were already waiting. "I'm just like them," Miranda thought. Only Jacobina looked out of place here. They brought Miranda a pile of magazines that she couldn't read.

"Mrs. Markowitz," the receptionist called.

Mrs. Markowitz closed the magazine she was leafing through, adjusted her soft-leather shoulder bag, and stood up.

✳   ✳   ✳

But one-hundred thousand dollars was not enough money for John Xuárez. The office space his mother bought for him turned out to be too small. He also needed an extra secretary and a partner and a vice-president of construction and an accountant. He even thought of hiring a full-time attorney, but left that for later. It was too expensive. And one computer wasn't enough either. He wanted to computerize the whole business, so he sold his office space for any price he could get, because it was supposedly a buyer's market, and got a mortgage for a twelve-thousand square-foot office in a brand new building on Brickell Avenue.

The corner office with a fantastic view of Biscayne Bay was for John Xuárez, the President. He kept three of the ten new computers for himself and got an eight-thousand dollar loan for brand new expensive office furniture. He then took a partner, not so much for his money, but for his talent, and offered him sixty-thousand dollars a year and a company car. A worried Miranda paid for all that, but she quickly calmed down and convinced herself that John probably knew what he was doing. She loved her son deeply, madly, blindly. He wasn't always kind to her and didn't even let her participate in the business as she had expected, but that was all right, John knew what he was doing; he said it would look bad if he had his mother working for him. Besides, she didn't even speak English. And why was she poking around in his bills? Didn't she trust him? All she had to do was sit back and relax. He'd take care of the business.

"But, John!" Miranda would say when he told her to go, once again, into debt.

"Mom! Hasn't Xuárez Construction made money from the very beginning?"

Indeed it had. Right away John had gotten several remodeling projects. So he probably knew what he was doing...

Did his partner need to make that much money though? And did John need a salary of at least a hundred-and-fifty thousand dollars a year in order to make ends meet?

"Do you want to be rich or don't you?" John asked his mother.

"Of course I do, John," Miranda replied. "I always wanted you to become a general contractor."

"Well, you have to spend money in order to make money," John finally convinced his mother. He probably knew what he was doing. He was so intelligent; he said this business was a golden goose.

Before long, Jacqueline joined him. She was the computer expert and took a different computer seminar every week.

"John, aren't these computer seminars a little expensive?" Miranda protested shyly.

"We're the business of the future, Mom," John answered. "Please, Mom, I'm busy now."

"O.K., I'll leave, but first give me a kiss!"

"Mom, please, you're really bothering me."

Oh, she loved him so much! Her son. He was so handsome! They didn't come any handsomer. And intelligent, too. She'd do anything for him. And no need to worry. He knew what he was doing. He was her son, and not at all like his father. Jacqueline was like him, too, but Miranda didn't really get along with Jacqueline.

"Why do you let her work with you and not me?" Miranda asked John.

"Mom! She's young! Look in the mirror! Plastic surgery really hasn't done anything for you. And I want my business to have a young, dynamic look. Pardon the expression, but no room for grandmothers here!"

"Jacqueline isn't that pretty," Miranda argued. "You should've seen me at her age!"

"Mom, please, I don't want to hear about the good old days!"

Miranda was jealous of Jacqueline, and almost treated her as if she were a daughter-in-law. As to Kiki, Miranda didn't even want to think about her; she was just like her father.

Soon the remodeling projects got to be too menial for Xuárez Construction Co. John decided to reorganize the company and this reorganization meant letting go of all the small projects and concentrating on multi-million dollar contracts. John Xuárez suddenly wanted to compete with the big-name construction companies. He even dreamt of becoming a monopoly and selling stock, appearing on The Wall Street journal, going public.

"But John, those little projects are bringing you a lot of money," Miranda argued shyly.

"I'm a man of the future, Mom," John retorted. "Or do you want me to be like my father?"

"No. Not at all. Your father was a man everyone took advantage of, and I don't want that for my son. But how are you going to survive if you let go of all the remodeling projects?"

"According to my calculations, the big contracts will start coming in in approximately six months. We'll just have to put a second mortgage on your house."

"I hope you know what you're doing, John."

"Listen, Mom, there are people dying to get in on this. It was just to do you a favor so you could participate, but if you don't trust me, just say so and we'll become like strangers. I'll never ask you a favor again!"

"No, I didn't mean it that way, John. Please, don't get mad, John!"

"I really hate it when you give me shit, Mom."

"I won't. I promise I won't anymore. But please don't get mad at me. Give me a kiss!"

"Please, Mom! I'm busy! This is business!"

They had everything and owned nothing. But it was so easy. The system was so good to them. You want a mansion?

Here, take it. You want a loan on the loan that you just got? Why didn't you ask before? A new car? Another new car? A condo for John?

"You really made it," Jacobina told her sister when she was visiting one winter.

"I told you I would," Miranda replied. "And how are things in Elizabeth?"

"The same. Always the same. Except that I finally bought that little house. Do you ever think about it?"

"No."

"Anyway. Why would you? What a silly question! And I rent the basement and the second floor out," Jacobina said, holding back the tears.

"Jacobina, why are you crying?"

"It's Carlos!" Jacobina broke down.

"Why, why, why? What's wrong with Carlos?"

"He wants to get married! He met this horrible woman named Silvia Bos, and I hate her. She's already been married, and I didn't put my son through college so he could get a second-hand girl. I put him through college," Jacobina wept and wept, "so he could have the best. Not a second-hand girl. That Silvia Bos, I hate her! I hate her!"

"Oh, my God! You're saying that he wants to marry a divorced woman?! If John ever wants to do that, I'll shoot her! He'd break my heart to pieces! And I thought he was breaking my heart now! Oh, Jacobina, I pity you. I'd hate to be in your position. I hope John never wants to do that!"

But that is not how John Xuárez broke his mother's heart. The blow came from where Miranda least expected it. John turned out to be just like her. Almost a caricature of her. She sowed, and then she reaped. Or was it the system? Miranda quickly blamed it on the system. It couldn't have been her son, not John. He knew what he was doing. He was born a businessman. No, John wasn't at all like his father. It couldn't have been John, so it was definitely the system.

Suddenly the system, that same system that up to then had been so good to them and had satisfied their every whim, suddenly that system changed its mind. Like an Indian giver, it began taking everything back. At first it didn't really matter; it was only Jacqueline's car, and the problem was solved overnight. She got a cheaper car. Then the system wanted John's car. But how could John thrive and survive without a

luxury vehicle? What?! The computers now?! How can you run
a business without computers? John threw his arms up in the
air. He absolutely refused to be the president of a Mom-and-
Pop business, so he threatened to abandon everything if
Miranda didn't do something right away. It was all her fault
anyway. She never had liked his partner. And if John couldn't
have his partner and his computers and his corner office and
his secretaries, he simply preferred to give up, go into something else, something easy like real estate. Anyway, the general-contracting business was no good, he solemnly declared
and repeated every day. The interest rates were too high.
Real estate was where the money was, he had this hunch. In
October they couldn't make the payroll, and John didn't even
go to the office anymore. He said he needed a vacation. He
told his mother to sell that office space for any price she could
get since it was a buyer's market. But how can you sell something you don't own? "Mom! I thought the office was all paid
off!"

"But where was I going to get the money, John?"

"You got me into general contracting, now get me out of
it!"

The system wanted the office back anyway; they didn't
even have to bother trying to sell it. Wanted to put someone
else in there perhaps? Some other company? And the system
wanted John's condo back. And the system wanted Miranda's
car back.

"Tell me what to do, John!" Miranda begged.

"I don't know, Mom. Get a job."

"There's no justice in this country!" Miranda yelled.
"Everything was so much better in Cuba! If only Fidel hadn't
taken over! Tomás would still be alive and we'd have nothing
to worry about! There is no justice in this country! I just can't
wait for the day when I'll be able to return to Cuba and
reclaim all my property!"

"Mom, please go scream elsewhere."

"O.K., but give me a kiss. How long has it been since you
last gave me a kiss?"

"Mom, please!"

They lost everything, and Tomás wasn't even there to
take the blame for it. John fled to Costa Rica and decided to
stay there until "things cooled down." There were several
warrants against him. Jacqueline, in turn, met a guru and

fled to New York City. She said she had never really been
interested in the construction business anyway.

Before boarding the plane that would take her to
Newark, New Jersey, Miranda went to the bank and handed
in the keys to her house. She no longer had a car. She landed
in Newark with $150 in her wallet. That was all she had. And
the cab to Elizabeth cost her twenty dollars.

Her sister Jacobina was feeling much better. Although
Carlos had married Silvia Bos, he had finally "seen the light,"
realized "how cheap she really was," and "dumped her." They
were divorced now. And these days Jacobina's existence
underwent a tragic experience every time Carlos met some
new woman and fell in love because nobody was good enough
for Carlos. But at least Jacobina knew how to solve these dra-
matic problems now. She'd become an expert after all these
years, especially since Carlos had this tendency to fall in love
easily and blindly. All it took on her part was a little trip to
the *botánica*, the witchcraft store in downtown Elizabeth, and
patient hatred on her part for the next couple of weeks. In little or no time, the latest second-hand girl was, as she said,
"history."

Winter came. Miranda was working nights and weekends
cleaning offices in Secaucus, New Jersey. All her co-workers
were illegal aliens and she'd listen to their stories of how they
had come into this country with someone else's visa and passport. They missed their children, their husbands, their country, their families, and Miranda comforted them when they
wept. She would assure them that everything would turn out
fine and add that if she were still rich, she'd help them as best
she could. She wished she had known before. And she was
sincere. Profoundly so.

It was a very cold winter. One Wednesday in the afternoon, Miranda accompanied Jacobina to the *botánica* in
downtown Elizabeth. Carlos had fallen in love with Silvia Bos'
cousin, of all people, and Jacobina was determined to do
something about that. Another one of these "second-hand
girls" she had to get rid of. A black chicken would do it. Little
did it matter how much it cost.

Jacobina Flecha walked out of the *botánica* and held the
door open for her sister, Miranda Xuárez. Miranda kept
warning Jacobina that what she was doing was wrong. "You
can't spend your life hating Carlos' girlfriends, Jacobina. God

will punish you. Please listen to what I'm saying, or you'll
punish yourself. And the more you get away with it, the more
severe the punishment will be." It was so cold outside! And
the static! But Miranda didn't worry about her hair anymore.
No more Jacqueline Kennedy hairdos. She didn't even dye it
anymore. Just left it gray. As a matter of fact, she didn't even
think about Jacqueline Kennedy anymore. They had both
grown old and Miranda's heart was weak now. Instead of
spending her money on cosmetics, she spent it on medicine to
moderate her blood pressure.

"Well, I hope you never put a curse on me," she told
Jacobina.

"I don't get angry at you anymore," Jacobina replied casually. "There's no reason to get angry at you. Somehow you
were forgiven. And I don't even know why."

They waited for five minutes at the bus stop. But it was
unbearably cold. So they sought refuge in the cafeteria next to
the old Dutch church and ordered two cups of coffee. They'd
run out of there the minute they saw the bus. This does not
happen often. Miranda had already returned to that same
cafeteria, but she hadn't remembered, perhaps because all the
elements weren't there, perhaps because she had returned on
a summer day, or on a Friday, or in the morning, perhaps
because there was no static electricity and she couldn't
remember, perhaps because she hadn't been ready to remember all those other times she had returned to this cafeteria in
downtown Elizabeth. But suddenly she did remember what
she'd lost. She felt this pressure on her neck and touched it
lightly with her finger. There would probably be another
black and blue mark there now, from the high blood pressure.
Lately the black and blue marks just popped up, and she did-
n't even have to hurt herself. They suddenly appeared either
on her face, or on her arms, her legs, her neck. And she wasn't
thinking of the house in Bal Harbour, or of the luxury cars,
the Louis Vuitton handbags, the Bal Harbour Shops where
she'd spend in cosmetics what she barely made now in a
month. She remembered Tomás. She'd never really ever
thought about him. Not even when he was alive. She remembered that last time. "Was it twenty-two years ago, Jacobina?"
Tomás had just been offered a teaching position at the Academy of the Assumption. And he was happy, because this made
her happy, and he loved her. She was remembering that time,

when she was sitting right here, in this cafeteria in downtown
Elizabeth, and without knowing it she was happy. Because
she'd see Tomás that very same day, and she could have
kissed him, and held his hand if she had wanted to. But she
never had (she had actually thought she didn't love him!). Too
late for regret though; it could even kill her. And Kiki was in
trouble, so Miranda had to keep on living. No, no regret, what
mattered were these empty sidewalks of Elizabeth. How
warm they seemed and how special that moment was, reminding her of Tomás and how much he had loved her, and
that once, a long time ago, a long time ago....

"What are you thinking about, Miranda?"

"What I lost."

ONCE IN A LIFETIME
OFFERING

That evening there was a debate on tv because a woman was running for the Vice-Presidency. Kiki wasn't the least bit interested in politics. She sat on the homely couch, pulled Section 9 out of the Sunday Times, and weighed it with her hand. There seemed to be many jobs in there.

Jamie, one of her roommates, was sitting in the easy chair. She had her legs tucked underneath her, a can of Diet Pepsi in her hand, and her eyes glued to the tv set. From her comments, it seemed as if the whole intellectual future of this country depended on the outcome of this debate. Kiki didn't agree with her. She insisted that Democrats and Republicans were one and the same, so what difference would it make? "You think that because you're Cuban," Jamie declared. "For Cubans the political world is either Red or non-Red, but this here is history, Kiki."

Four girls, Kiki, Sharon, Jamie, and Kathryn, were sharing the downstairs part of a house on Ogden Avenue in Jersey City Heights. Sharon and Jamie were both twenty-nine, while Kathryn and Kiki were, in help-wanted terms, recent grads. Jeff, the owner of the house, lived upstairs and rented the lower floor out. He was a poet, a proofreader, and a landlord at the same time. After a brief affair with Jamie, Jeff had turned to Kathryn three months before, the day Kathryn had moved into this house with Kiki, her best friend from college. But somehow Kiki had fallen in love with Jeff, and she could no longer tolerate Kathryn's presence. Not only that, but the response to her resumés hadn't exactly been what she had expected. Kiki, who had thought that New York City had been eagerly waiting for her to graduate, hadn't gotten one single telephone call as of yet. So her heart was bleeding.

On Monday morning, Kiki was again overflowing with positive resolutions and enthusiasm. She decided to get organized and to be strong and courageous. It was no use being depressed. Talking with Sharon always did her a lot of good. Sharon was absolutely right when she said, "I know you're intelligent. You know you're intelligent. But nobody out there does. So you have to prove it to them. And you won't get anywhere by moping in your bedroom." After they both agreed that the most important thing was a positive attitude, they decided that for the time being—since Kiki hadn't gotten any responses to her letters and resumés as of yet—and only for the time being Kiki's best bet would be to go to an employment agency, just so she wouldn't have to put up with her mother and keep asking her for money.

Kiki turned to the College-Grad columns in the help-wanted section and immediately chanced upon an ad that seemed to have been written for her and her only. In bold letters it read "I didn't go to college to type." Below, the small type said that there was life after college, the fun didn't have to stop there, the possibilities were endless. It even said: "please" call...Kiki's heart was pounding. She could barely wait until nine a.m. Oh, this was great! She had a quick breakfast with Sharon and Jamie who were both moaning, "Shit, it's Monday morning," and waited until they were gone to wash her hair and to dress. At ten past nine she was dialing the number of CareerCareers! this fabulous employment agency that actually cared. They told her to come in as quickly as possible to fill out an application. So it was all a matter of attitude! She took the bus to the Hoboken Path station and reflected. She felt like a brand new person!

The offices of CareerCareers! were on Fifth Avenue in midtown Manhattan. Kiki Xuárez took the elevator to the twelfth floor. For a minute she was disappointed that so many other people were getting off on the same floor as she was, but she quickly refused to let this bother her. These people's backgrounds were probably completely different from hers, Besides, CareerCareers! seemed to have many jobs to offer, so these people here weren't necessarily competing with her. Manhattan was a big place, she thought as she stood in line at the reception desk. There were exactly eight people in front of her. She opened her briefcase and took out her resumé. Her feet hurt. The line was moving quickly. A woman in a bad mood handed her an application form, told her to fill it out, then come back. Kiki said she didn't need one; she'd brought her resumé along. Then the woman in a bad mood told her that everyone else had brought their resumé and still had to fill out an application form. Then Kiki wondered if she had been standing in the right line, for she was, after all, a college grad and all her teachers had praised her and respected her and told her about the great future that was awaiting her. Actually, Kiki thought she had already "made it" the day her diploma was handed to her. So why did her feet hurt? And why was she filling out this application form like everybody else? Maybe these other people didn't even have Master's degrees..."Excuse me." She went to the woman in a bad mood and said, "was this the line for the college grads?"

"Everyone here's a college grad," the woman grunted.

"Your attitude," Kiki thought to herself. "Think positive. If not, they'll get bad vibes." She continued fighting against disappointment and childish humiliation as she wrote Enriqueta Xuárez on the dotted line. And her address, her number, city, state. Work experience. College newspaper. College art gallery. Great with people. A people-person. Self starter. Organized. Always on time. References. And they only asked for three names. But she had more than three names. All her teachers would put in a good word for her. She should put Mr. Richardson first; he had published many articles on literature of the Georgian era and was probably famous. CareerCareers! was probably going to be impressed. Was she name-dropping? But she was so proud of her diploma! Suddenly Kiki started imagining one of the CareerCareers! counselors walking out of his office and shouting out, "Who's Enriqueta Xuárez?!" She'd timidly raise her hand and he'd say, "God, you mean you actually worked under Richardson?! Wow! Can't believe it! That's fantastic! Come into my office. You shouldn't be wasting your time out here!"

She then began filling out the part about her background. In the box where it said "graduated," Kiki felt like writing "of course." After having checked to see if the xerox copies of her Master's degree were in her briefcase and put NA in the last section of the application form where they asked about other skills such as typing, word processing and what not, she stood up and walked to the reception desk.

The woman in a bad mood put her application form at the bottom of a tall pile and crudely told her to go and sit down and wait till she was called for her typing test. Kiki told her she must be mistaken, for she wasn't applying for a clerical position. "Still have to take a typing test," the woman said.

"But I don't know how to type," Kiki protested.

"Have to take it anyway. Some jobs only require light typing. Next!" the woman yelled, and turned to another hungry job-hunter who also had a question.

Forty-five minutes later Kiki was still waiting. She was getting impatient and irritated and even thought about walking out of there, but she immediately reminded herself of the conversation she had had with Sharon the night before. "I know you're intelligent. YOU know you're intelligent. But the rest of the world...why should the rest of the world know?" Sharon's words soothed Kiki, and before long the imaginary CareerCareers! counselor was out there again looking for her. You mean to say you worked under Richardson?! Wow! Come into my office. You're wasting your time out here. How long have you been waiting? And to think we've kept somebody who worked under Richardson waiting! Interested in International Affairs? Dealing with high dignitaries? Are you a bright, aggressive, self-motivated individual? Then I've got a job for you!

"Enrico Cuarez!" Kiki heard, and the imaginary Career-Careers! counselor suddenly disappeared. "Enriqueta Xuárez," Kiki corrected the woman who was calling her. Here was her typing test, and she could practice for ten minutes then call her. Her counselor, Trish was her name, she'd set up the timer, Kiki would have exactly five minutes, not a second more. Any questions?

Kiki scored 20 w.p.m on her typing test. An hour later, she heard her name being called again. It was her turn for an interview. "I'm Trish," the CareerCareers! counselor said to her again. So her typing wasn't too good, but perhaps she'd have something for Kiki. Just a temporary assignment though, but temping was pretty good, "especially while you job shop," Trish said. This was just a one-day assignment though. No, no typing involved. Good with figures? Mostly research-oriented. Show up at the Time-Life Building tomorrow at eight a.m. Ask for Mike and he'll get you started. Have to look corporate, though. Well-groomed. Lipstick. What you're wearing now won't do. Too casual. It pays $3.25 an hour. Trish rose and said, "Good luck! Come back here on Wednesday, and we'll work from there."

"Thank you very much!" Kiki said.

So she had her first job. In the Time-Life Building! And she had to look corporate! And no typing involved! Almost too good to be true. Only for a day, though. But maybe they'd like her and want to keep her on. You studied under Richardson?! Wow! And what was your thesis about? The supposed tyranny of Alexander Pope?! His relation to the poetry of the latter half of the eighteenth century?! About Pope's authority that remained intact until the arrival of the new potentates, Wordsworth, Coleridge, Scott, and Byron?! Have we got a job for you! Are you prompt and personable? Can you work under pressure? Then you fit the bill. We're going to put your knowledge of literature of the Georgian era to good use!

That evening at home Kiki was bursting with enthusiasm. She bragged to Sharon and Jamie about how she'd found a job in little or no time. It had been so easy! And in the Time-Life Building of all places! It was really too bad that Kathryn had practically moved in with Jeff and that nobody down here had seen her for the past five days, because Kiki would have simply loved to brag to her. Kiki even made up a little speech in her mind which included everything she was dying to say to Kathryn. Kathryn! Where's your sense of responsibility? Why aren't you out there in the world struggling and fighting like I am? Where did our college resolutions go? We have to stand by them, you know. Perhaps that job at the Time-Life Building was only a one-day job, but you never know what can happen in a day. Besides, from what Kiki's CareerCareers! counselor had said, this was a high visibility position.

Tuesday morning was hectic. Kiki was so excited that she barely slept all night, then fell into a deep sleep at five in the morning. She almost overslept! Or the alarm didn't go off. Either that or she turned it off. So when she opened her eyes it was half-past six. And she had to be there at eight! She showered and dressed and put her makeup on as quickly as she could. At ten to seven she was running to Manhattan Avenue to catch either the mini-bus or the 99S. But it was raining! And her feet hurt! While waiting for the bus, she took out a little pocket mirror in order to inspect her face. She looked atrocious! Her foundation was smeared here and there! Oh! Why was life so difficult? And it was raining, and she had forgotten her umbrella, and her feet hurt. She had these water-filled blisters all over her feet because of the high-heeled pumps she had bought for the job hunting. They'd seemed so comfortable when she first tried them on in the store. Now she had these blisters with a watery substance inside, and they hurt even more when she popped them, and she'd already popped several of them.

It turned out to be a high-visibility job indeed. They sat her on the fourteenth floor and told her to count the number of people who walked in and out of elevators one through four. An elevator company was doing a survey. By noon, she was so depressed that she stopped counting and put anything on her tally sheet. She remembered her college days in New England. It had only been five months since she'd graduated, but Kiki the student now seemed to belong to a distant past. Up on that fourteenth floor of the Time-Life Building, she had this sudden vision of springtime in Massachusetts when everyone was lying on the grass studying for the finals. How beautiful the campus was in spring! And what a delightful atmosphere. Flowers and hopes and dreams. So quiet at times, when everyone was having lunch in the cafeteria and she would have her solitary picnic on the grass. Bite into her sandwich while she read *Pamela*, take a sip of Seven Up, and continue with *The Castle of Otranto*. Or put her handbag under her head and Pope's *Essay on Man* on her chest. Was it all finished now? Didn't New York City want her?

"That was a disgusting, humiliating job," Kiki told Sharon that evening. There was yet another debate on tv. It seemed as if the Democrats would win. They were having chicken for dinner. Jamie had prepared it with Shake and Bake. "Oh, I'm so depressed," Kiki said.

"Just hang in there, girl!" Sharon insisted. "It took me nearly a year to get my job, which isn't even that great a job…I know what you're going through. Temping is depressing."

"Me, too, I hate temping," Jamie said during the commercial break.

"What am I going to do with my life?" Kiki wondered out loud.

* * *

It turned out that a woman did not become Vice President of the United States. And on election day Kathryn finally decided to come downstairs. She told her roommates that she had been doing a lot of thinking during this past month and had decided to go for an M.B.A.

"You must be crazy!" Jamie exclaimed.

"It's supposed to be real boring," Sharon warned her.

"Yeah, but it's the only way to make any money," Kathryn argued. "Look at you girls, both twenty-nine and barely taking two-hundred dollars a week home. That sucks!"

"But what about literature?" Kiki asked suddenly. "Didn't you make some kind of commitment to literature? What's the use of studying Byron if you're going to turn around and study business administration after that?"

"I bet you're really putting your knowledge of literature of the Georgian era to good use at the Daylight Savings Bank!" Kathryn snapped at Kiki. "Besides, I think I've outgrown literature."

"Now I've heard everything!" Sharon said. "So you've decided to become a shallow yuppie now that you've outgrown literature . . . Kathryn, you haven't even tried!"

"Well, Sharon," Kathryn replied, "I don't think I need to try. I've just taken a good look at the battlefield from my Jersey City Heights window, and you know what I noticed? I noticed that you've been trying for five years, and where has it gotten you? Oh, you're going to say that you're working at Gallows. People kill, cheat, lie, and steal to work at Gallows. Good for you! I hope you're happy with that little assistant's job. Oh, and why don't you tell me what you do all day? Make xerox copies? Nice. Type business letters? Sweet! Tell me, what are the other profound things that you do all day? All those things that give you the good conscience of not being a shallow yuppie? And allow you to sleep well at night knowing that you'll have to rush out of here the next morning in order to get a few peanuts on Friday? And you want me to try?! Sharon, you can't tell the difference between the road less traveled and a dead-end street!"

For the past two weeks Kiki had been working at the Daylight Savings Bank on West 33rd Street. The hours were eight-to-five with an hour break for lunch that wasn't included in her workday because when she went to lunch she had to punch out. But at least she was working and could scramble up her share of the rent and chip in for the food and still have a little pocket money left. At least she didn't have to ask her parents for help after they had spent all that money to put her through one of the best universities in the country. Every month her father sent her a hundred dollars in traveler's checks, though. It always came in handy because she had to count every penny, and an extra soda at the cafeteria could mean having to borrow money the next day in order to get to work. He also included a letter in the envelope where he begged her not to tell her mother about this. She knew her mother, he wrote, and this could upset her. He also added that he was very proud of her.

Kiki was not happy. Working in a cubbyhole at the Daylight Savings Bank even for this short period of time was draining her. The worst part of it was that she never even got to see the light of day. The administrative offices of the Daylight Savings Bank were in a gigantic square building in a gloomy neighborhood. The windows were reserved for the important people. So walking through the corridors of this building resembled strolling through an exclusive beach resort. All the mansions were in front of the ocean and behind high walls. You never got to see the water. Every morning was a mad rush to get there and punch in at nine a.m. Since it was winter, she would arrive at work before sunrise, and since the neighborhood was dreary and there was a cafeteria inside the building, she never even bothered to go out at lunchtime. Of course, the cafeteria with the windows was reserved for the important people. Not even at lunchtime did she see what the day looked like.

They gave her a cubbyhole, but she hardly ever got to sit. Her supervisor, having noticed right away that she stuffed envelopes quickly and precisely, decided to send her to the filing department. This was where all the important papers such as deeds, liens, and wills were kept. And it was hectic in there. When she arrived in the morning, there were at least fifty files that had to be put back in their respective drawers. They used a very convoluted filing system with letters and numbers. Kiki caught on right away, and they were happy with her. She was sharp. But this was like raking leaves in autumn. Whenever she was down to her last five files, sixty more arrived. No sense of accomplishment. In a week's time, Kiki had paper cuts all over her hands. The following week her cuticles were so bloody that she was getting blood on the precious files. She decided to quit at the end of the third week, after having talked to someone who had been back there in that bleak filing room for twenty years. It was Christmas time anyway, and she wanted to go to Miami to visit her family.

"Well?" her mother said.

"Well, what?"

"Don't get sassy, Kiki. You're so temperamental. When do you intend to get a good job?"

"I'm trying, Mom."

"It's no use going to the university if it's to live in New Jersey and make less than four dollars an hour. Sometimes trying isn't enough."

"Well, Mom, for your information, it's pretty hard to get a good job whether you go to the university or not. But when I get back, I'm going to have a completely different attitude. I swear. I'm never going to get depressed again or despair. I'm just going to go for it, I swear, Mom. That's my resolution for the new year."

"Kiki, have you ever thought about teaching?" her father asked. "If I were you, I'd think about getting a Ph.D. Teaching can be a very rewarding career."

"Sure!" her mother yelled. "Let's put a mortgage on the house so she can go study some more and drain us out of our last penny! Now a Master's degree isn't enough, it only gives you three dollars an hour. Now the child needs a Ph.D.! She has to spend her life studying while we're here bleeding ourselves! And how much will she earn with a Ph.D.? Four? No, no, no! No way! The problem with this child is that she has no drive, no courage, no ambition! She thinks her parents are millionaires! Well, we're not, for her information. With the education she has, it's obscene that she's not making a fortune by now! Look at Jacobina's son!" She was shouting at the top of her lungs now. "He's more than aware of the sacrifice his mother made for him. Every day, rain or shine, I see children who've made it and didn't have a tenth of what this child here had! And the Chávez children! They cleaned toilets in Harvard! Now they're supporting their parents!"

✳ ✳ ✳

In January, upon her return to New York, Kiki was determined to get an interesting job with a decent salary. "Why don't you look in the bilingual section?" Sharon suggested. "You're Cuban. You speak Spanish fluently. Maybe you'll find something interesting there."

"That's a great idea!" Kiki exclaimed. "Why didn't I think of it before?! They really need bilingual people, don't they?"

The bilingual ads looked good. There was even this agency, the Bi Agency, that bragged about its "Bi Counselors" who spoke your language. They had over one hundred immediate job openings. All you had to do was choose your field: Fashion/Cosmetics, Banking/Publ. Rel., Publishing, Entertainment. Plus, free in-house brush-up facilities! One of the Bi counselors sent Kiki to an interview with an engineering firm in Rockefeller Center. But they needed 70 w.p.m. typing, and although Kiki had tried for the past three weeks, she was only up to 40 w.p.m. now.

The Bi counselor reassured her. She shouldn't worry; the first job interview was like the first pancake. And, as a matter of fact, there was a brand new opening that had just come in, a brand new opening, and perhaps she'd fit the bill. The Bi counselor took out an old wrinkled index card and read: import/export, lite typing, lite phones, lite billing, will train, Spanish helpful, hourly salary, no benefits, slow pace.

They set up an interview for the next day. The place was called The Malinche Volcano. They imported clothes, jewelry, and anything from Peru and Mexico. The offices were in a loft in the West twenties. Kiki was to see the owner of the company, Sara Saralegui, and "good luck!" the Bi counselor said. "Report to me after the interview," he added. "We'll take it from there."

A tall, beautiful, ageless woman opened the door.

"Hi! I'm Kiki Xuárez from the Bi Agency...I have an interview with Sara Saralegui."

"Oh, was it today?! I'm her," she said. "Come in, you must be kidding. Is your name really Kiki?! I hope you're not one of those Latinos who refuse to speak Spanish. I'm prejudiced against them. Sit down. Is your name really Kiki? That is so queer! I say that because my boyfriend's name is also Kiki. You'll meet him. Not today. I'm mad at him. He's a real bastard. I swear I don't give a shit about his sciatica. I hope they told you the pay wasn't very good. One thing about this company, we're always losing money. And I mean, we've been going downhill ever since we started. By we I mean me. I don't even know why the hell I say we. Nobody here to help me. Kiki, and I don't mean you, has his wives and his shady business, and I don't really care what he does or count on him. Anyway, he doesn't help me at all. I'm not going to become one of his aunts. Swear to God I'm not. As to Sara, my daughter, she's seventeen. You'll meet her. All she ever does is get high and bad grades and bring men like Kiki home. She's the one who met him first, and I said no way; this one's for me. He's absolutely luscious though, I swear to God. A real bastard, but I swear he is something. Can't get enough of him, swear to God, and I'm difficult. Anyway, I'd like for you to handle the billing because I'm really up to here and I can't teach you how to do it 'cause I'm sick of it. So you figure it out. Just sit here. The kitchen table's as good as any table, and I hope you don't mind the yelling and the screaming. I'm absolutely furious at my daughter today. If you have any questions, please figure it out by yourself."

"Should I call the Bi Agency and tell them you've hired me?"

"Oh, no. Don't call those bastards! It's taken them a year to find someone for me. I'll just pay you directly."

So Kiki was left to herself with several long years' worth of neglected numbers on the kitchen table. Sara rushed to another room, closed the door, and began to yell. "Sara listen to me!" she hollered. And mother and daughter argued and called each other horrible names all day. Since the two Saras practically had the same voice, this heated argument sounded like one long monologue. As to Kiki, she had principles, and it was supposedly impolite to eavesdrop, so she shut her ears and didn't hear a thing, just the screaming. She refused to try to make sense of the words that were being said. She worked and worked and added and subtracted to the sound of this broken record of a nasty argument. She even forgot to take a break for lunch, engrossed as she was with her new job. It was much better than Daylight Savings, so she wanted Sara to be happy with her. In the middle of the afternoon, the angry Sara voices suddenly died down and it it got so quiet that it seemed as if a leopard were walking through the jungle. Mother or daughter opened the door; they both walked out of what was probably a bedroom, but Kiki didn't want to spy on them, so she didn't look. When she did look, the two Saras had their arms wrapped around each other.

"Oh! You're still here!" exclaimed Sara. "This is my daughter, Sara. I told you you'd meet her. Sara, guess what her name is. No, don't guess, it's Kiki!"

"Kiki! God, how queer!"

Kiki couldn't decide which one of the two Saras was prettier, or more voluptuous, or taller. So there was nothing to distinguish one Sara from the other, except that one of them was, obviously, older because she was the mother.

"Oh, my God, you got so much work done!" Sara exclaimed. "Good! Pretty good! Will you come back?"

"If you want me to," Kiki replied. "Tomorrow?"

"Yeah. Whenever you wake up. Just come in. You know where the work is."

"What are the hours?" Kiki asked.

"We don't have hours. Just work until you're tired or tired of it."

Kiki decided she was tired. She began tidying up, but Sara told her to leave everything the way it was. It was no use... Kiki stood up. It was time for the formal "have a good evening and see you tomorrow," but the two Saras were hugging and kissing each other. Kiki preferred not to interrupt them. She quietly closed the door behind her.

⁕ ⁕ ⁕

"So how's your new job?" Jamie asked.

"Strange. But I think I like it."

"You do? Little Miss Negative likes something? What kind of job is it?"

"I think I'm the bookkeeper of an import/export company."

"Bookkeeper! Yuk!

"Actually, it's not that bad," Kiki said.

"Sounds really strange coming from you. You're always so bitter."

"I'm not bitter, Jamie!" Kiki snapped. "It's just that I have to prove myself and justify my existence, and so far nobody's even let me get on the battlefield!"

That night in bed, Kiki thought about her resumé. She had spent the past seven months of her life going through the classified ads. Canned phrases such as "get your foot in the door" and "exceptional opportunity" crossed her mind. Creative. Fast-paced. THIS IS FOR YOU. A job you can sink your teeth into. She was half-asleep. Looking to hire a bright agressive individual. Only career-directed candidate need apply. Must be articulate, organized, and versed in corporate demeanor. And those other jobs, they wanted experience, a girl with her foot in the door already, that had her foot in the door, in the door. She dreamt about feet and doors. She thought about putting survey and research work for Abramson Elevator Co. and The Daylight Savings Bank. Now there was a new addition to the list: The Malinche Volcano. Administrative assistant? Translator? Market research? That's what she'd put! Market research. Still didn't have her foot in the door, though, in the door, this foot. Nobody out there cares about literature of the Georgian era.

She got to work at ten the next morning. "Oh, you're here early," a sleepy Sara Saralegui said. "Please don't get here this early. I'm going back to bed," she added, walked toward the bedroom, and closed the door behind her. Kiki worked steadily and quietly until noon when Sara emerged from her bedroom. "The witch's in school today," Sara said. "I'll make you lunch. Don't you think my daughter's a real bitch? How old are you?" she asked and opened the refrigerator.

"Twenty-four," Kiki replied.

"And a little *nya nya*," Sara said casually while she was rummaging in the refrigerator. "Can't find shit in here! You're a little *nya nya*, aren't you? Here it is! I'm heating up some soup."

"I don't know what you mean," Kiki said.

"About being *nya nya*? Never mind. Ever heard of Malinche?"

"No. Why?"

"Ever heard of Cortés?"

"Yes, of course I've heard of Cortés," Kiki replied. "I'm even supposed to be a descendant of his, but maybe the whole thing's a lie. Big deal. Sorry I mentioned that."

"Don't be sorry. Well, anyway," Sara started to explain, "Malinche was Cortés' interpreter. The minute she saw him, she fell in love with him. Or, in any case, that's what this man called Díaz says. Now here comes the interesting part. Three months later, when Cortés was trying to meet Moctezuma, he found out that Malinche spoke Nahuatl and that she was an Aztec who had been given to the Maya by her widowed mother. Anyway, to make a long story short," Sara carried on and it seemed as if she were gossiping about some acquaintances of hers, "I really wonder about this woman because she became his interpreter in three months. Now, you don't just learn a language in three months. It's as if you suddenly fell in love with the Japanese premier now, and you began interpreting for him by July. I know love conquers all, but doesn't that sound crazy to you? You know what I think? I think Malinche faked it. It was the easiest thing in the world to do. Not one Spaniard spoke Nahuatl and not one Aztec spoke Castilian, so Malinche could say whatever she wanted. So God knows what she told Moctezuma! Anyway, that's how Mexico was conquered. And it wasn't conquered because of the gold, it was conquered because one little woman was madly in love. Do you have a boyfriend?"

"No."

"Do you like men? Eat your soup."

"Of course I like men!" Kiki said. "I just haven't met the right one. Actually, I haven't even met one. Thank you for the soup."

"Wait until you meet Kiki, my boyfriend," Sara said. "You'll like him. He has the most beautiful hair in the world, and these black eyes . . . I wonder why people make such a big deal about blue eyes. I guess they just haven't looked into black eyes. You can barely see yourself in them. You'll like him! He's a real bastard though. He's been married one too many times, and his first wife, a Colombian who's around his age, forty, babysits for all the other children he's had since he dumped her! Isn't that outrageous? Anyway, you've had your lunch, please go now. Sara'll be back from school any minute and we're probably going to have a big fight and I don't want you to get involved in my personal life."

Three months later, Kiki was still working at The Malinche Volcano. Some days she would put in ten hours and at other times Sara would simply tell her to leave the minute she got there. As to the pay, it was as flexible as the hours. One week she'd take home four hundred dollars, fifty dollars the following week, and two hundred the week after that. It depended on Sara's mood on Fridays. Kiki didn't mind, and she actually looked forward to going to The Malinche Volcano. Jobwise it wasn't quite what she had expected, but it was much better than working at The Daylight Savings Bank, and it paid more, on an average. She continued job hunting, though. She was particularly attracted by the ads that read: willingness to travel 30% of the time, excellent written and oral skills, salary: $36-42K, the job demands a broad array of creative talents, and other challenging assignments, knowledge of Spanish a definite plus, rush resumé, clips, and salary history. Obviously, Kiki didn't have much of a salary history, but she continued getting enthusiastic each time she spotted an interesting ad, and every Monday morning she sent at least fifteen resumés out. By Friday she was wondering what was wrong with her. Not one single telephone call. Not ever. And she did despair often. But every Monday morning when she posted her resumés, she was filled with new hope and sure that this time someone would call her. It didn't happen.

"Ever heard of Malinche?" Sara asked.

"You're always asking me the same question, Sara."

"It's that I don't think I should have changed the name of my company because of her. Of course, I did that when I absolutely adored Malinche and really admired her because Cortés wouldn't have gotten anywhere without her. But these days I think I hate her. Or maybe it's Kiki, not you, who made me wonder about her. He thinks she was a traitor. You know, she was there when the Spaniards practically destroyed Tenochtitlán and desecrated the Aztec temples, and she just stood there and watched and helped Cortés destroy a whole civilization. And she was an Aztec herself! Isn't that outrageous? Here's an Aztec woman who thinks she's as Castilian as Queen Isabella. I really shouldn't have named my business after her. Well, look who's here! I'm so happy to see you. Kiss me! Kiss me! Kiki, did you meet Kiki?"

"No, I've never met him."

"I was talking to Kiki. This here is Kiki, your namesake."

He must have been six-foot-four. And that hair. That black hair. But nothing compared to the eyes. But nothing compared to his whole face. He was dressed in black and had on white tennis shoes and Kiki immediately thought that she had never ever ever seen anyone as handsome in her whole life and probably never would again in her whole lifetime, for he was incredible. He was, as Sara always said, absolutely luscious. What did she mean by that? So this was Kiki. Sara had told her that he had been married God knows how many times, and sometimes didn't even take the time to divorce,

and the first time it was to a Colombian woman. Was she
Colombian or Bolivian? Who cares?! That lucky woman! And
he had had two children with this first wife, and the second
time he'd married a Peruvian like himself with whom he had
had another two children. They then needed a live-in baby sit-
ter so they brought the first wife from Colombia or Bolivia to
live with them so she could take care of all the children. Then
he'd married a third time and had more children, and his first
wife was still taking care of all of them. And to think that she
had wasted her time being in love with Jeff all these months
when this man here existed.

"Well?" Kiki's mother said on the phone.

"Well, what?" Kiki replied, and she wished she could tell
her that she had just met this incredible man who had not
proposed to her. No, as a matter of fact he was already taken.
Yes, taken…it was best not to tell her about this man.

"When are you going to get a good job, child?" her mother
asked. "I don't even know what to tell the people here anymore. Kiki, I really don't want to be the laughingstock, and
everybody keeps asking me what kind of glamorous job you've
gotten since you graduated from that university that cost us
an arm and a leg, and I can't tell them you haven't found anything yet! I can't tell them you're crunching numbers for a
stupid little company nobody's even heard of! So what am I
going to tell them? Kiki, if I had known, or so much as suspected, that you were going to turn out to be this lazy, I never
would've spent all that money to send you to the university.
Look at your father! He's old; he deserves better than to see
you merely searching for a job and for yourself! Look at your
cousin Carlos! He's practically supporting his mother now!
Kiki, you have to stop and look around you!"

"I know, Mom, but I'm trying, I swear. Every Monday
morning I send out at least fifteen resumés, but I haven't gotten an answer yet."

"Kiki, I told you to study law. People who haven't got it in
them should always study law! You've already been in New
York for almost a year, and what have you done?"

These conversations with her mother always depressed
her. With a strange mixture of despair and anxiety and hope,
she'd go through the classified ads with a fine tooth comb.
Somebody in there had to want her! Three times she finally
succeeded in getting interviews, but she wanted these jobs

way too much. They always told her that they'd call her back, but they never did call back, did they? But during those weeks, when she anxiously awaited those phone calls and could almost hear the voice on the other side saying, "Congratulations, you've been hired!" she wouldn't stop talking to Jamie and Sharon about the job or jobs she'd soon have and wouldn't stop asking them what new clothes she should buy now that she was going to make a lot of money, wouldn't stop repeating that now, at last, she'd be doing her thing at last.

Sharon and Jamie witnessed her high hopes, the anxiety, the joy, the growing disappointment, and finally the despair over not having gotten a phone call. Kiki, Sara's boyfriend, always said, "all you need is the right soil to grow in." Sara knew, of course she did. From the beginning, Kiki had been sincere with her. So while Sara's boyfriend was telling her to find the right soil to grow in, Sharon and Jamie tried to comfort her. They even said, "Well, you're not even that miserable at The Malinche Volcano anyway."

Indeed, she wasn't. The minute Kiki walked into Sara's loft, she immediately forgot about herself and her desperate search for a job and worst of all her fear of failure. What if she never did find a way to justify her existence? During the whole month of May, Kiki even had dinner at The Malinche Volcano, not so much because she wanted to work late, but because Kiki, Kiki her namesake, would often be there. Sara didn't seem to mind. She said she was past jealousy and even kidded her about it. "So you're in love with Kiki!" Sara often said to her.

"Of course I'm not in love with Kiki," Kiki always protested. "He's sweet, that's all. And he makes me laugh. And he's handsome. And he's fun to be with. And when he talks to me...I have the impression I'm the most important thing in the world, as if nothing else existed. He's so available! But he's too eccentric. Sara, I swear, I'm not in love with him!"

It was only when she took her Path train back to New Jersey that Kiki remembered her job hunting, her uncertain future, her resumés that did not seem to impress anyone. She wondered what it was that they wanted. Experience? But where do you get experience if, to work, you have to have experience, and they won't give you work unless you have experience? What did they want? Clips? What was wrong with being a beginner anyway? Some beginners catch on right

away. Probably wanted to make their positions appear difficult. Humiliating if a beginner gets it right away. She had
even become an excellent bookkeeper in little or no time, and
that because Sara had given her the responsibility and practically ordered her to make all decisions herself.

"So, how do I get in?" she was still asking Jamie and
Sharon. "How do I get my foot in the door, as they say? All the
doors are bolted. Should I break in?"

"Do you think I have my foot in the door?" Jamie asked.
"It takes time."

"How much time?" Kiki was still asking. "A whole lifetime?"

"Kiki, you're depressing us," Sharon was still saying.

"She may have a point there," Ron, who was Sharon's
boyfriend, said.

"Maybe Kathryn's right," Kiki added. "Studying to get an
M.B.A. Struggling to break the door down."

"I don't want to hear this. You're depressing me," Sharon
stopped her right there. "Anyway, the only thing that matters
in life is being true to one's self, whether or not it makes you
happy. It'll make you happy in the long run."

"Kiki may have a point there," Ron repeated. "I mean, I
work my fingers to the bone in construction all day, and what
do I get in return? Time to read? The gentle feeling that I'm
being true to myself? I'm too tired to even think about being
true to myself. Or maybe we're all a bunch of ex-bookworms
with no talent whatsoever."

"Not you, too, Ron," Sharon stood up and shouted. "And
I'm going to bed, godamnit!"

*　*　*

The next day at work Sara asked, "Ever heard of Malinchism?"

"Of course I haven't," Kiki replied. "The word doesn't
even exist, and I don't want to talk today, I'm desperate and
depressed."

"Of course you're depressed," Sara said matter of factly.

"So are you going to tell me that I should cheer up and go
for it?"

"May my tongue burn in the filthy fires of hell if I ever
talk shit like that," Sara said casually. "Anyway, you can't go

for it if you're not ready. You don't even know what to go for, Kiki."

"Oh, yes, I do. I studied literature, and I love literature, and I just want the world to allow me to put this love to good use, that's all. I know what I want, Sara, I really do."

"And how come you didn't study your own literature?" Sara asked and sat on the kitchen table.

"You mean Hispanic literature? Because I don't like it. It bores me. I hate it. It doesn't concern me."

"Oh, but it does. Ever heard of Malinchism?"

"No, Sara, I've never heard of that word that doesn't exist," Kiki said, and two tears landed on Sara's ledgers.

"Well, I'll tell you about it just to cheer you up. You see, the Mexicans came up with that word because of Malinche. It's supposed to describe a social inferiority complex that makes you disdain everything that's yours, for example your country, your language, your people, etc....and prefer everything that's foreign. Take Malinche. The minute she met Cortés she began acting just like a Castilian woman and even calling herself Marina. Anyway, I was wondering if this Malinchism here could affect our whole person. Maybe you think that you can't succeed because you're you, that you can't get a job because you're you, and that everybody else can get somewhere precisely because they're not you. So I was just wondering, since you came from an unhappy family, and you insist on acting a hundred percent Anglo, and you're always falling in love with other women's men, and you have proven yourself incapable of landing a half-decent job, and your mother disdains you, I was just wondering if you hated yourself."

✳ ✳ ✳

Really, Kiki was happy at The Malinche Volcano, especially when she was there concentrating on her numbers, or chatting with that beautiful delightful Sara, or admiring that black-haired, black-eyed Kiki, her namesake, from a distance. These were the times she forgot all about her mother who was always calling up and asking, "Well?" And she also forgot about her friends who constantly repeated that she wasn't really trying. And, most important of all, these were the times she forgot about herself and that nagging, slimy feeling of failure, that terrible impression that she would never get that glamorous, high-paying job she and her mother dreamt about, and that she would never get anywhere in life if she...if she didn't?...just like her mother predicted.

Suddenly, in the middle of summer, her father died of a heart attack. Kiki packed all her bags and left for a three-month stay in Miami. Her mother was hysterical. Only the twins seemed to be taking this loss with some wisdom. They insisted that their father had led a good, full life, and that everyone has to die one day. As to Kiki, she thought she'd never stop crying. The despair over this loss was was so terrible that she could not even imagine life any other way now. It would be a valley of tears from now on, forever. She could never smile again. She even refused to leave her mother's house for a whole month because, at least there, she had grown accustomed to the things that reminded her of him. She knew how to beware. Don't let that chair in the kitchen surprise you or remind you of your father. But it was different out in the street where the street corners and the store windows could creep up on her and remind her that she'd never see him again.

Kiki was the last one in her family to return to a normal life. One afternoon her mother decided that it was time to stop mourning and that life had to go on. Immediately, she began asking Kiki what she intended to do with her life and warning her about how quickly the years passed. Before she knew it, she'd be...

It was in January of 1986 that Kiki returned to New York. She was more determined than ever to get that glamorous, prestigious, high-paying job that her mother had drilled into her heart because she wanted the best for her. Things had somewhat changed in Jersey City Heights. First of all Ron, Sharon's boyfriend, had moved in with them, and, from what Kiki heard, Kathryn, after having studied for her M.B.A. and outgrown literature, had also outgrown Jeff. She had moved out of Ogden Avenue and gotten a consultant's position at Gallows where Sharon worked and was living in Soho with some editor. Sharon was a bit upset because the day Kathryn walked into Gallows as a consultant, she was offered four times more money than her—Sharon, who had been working there for six years, who knew the company by heart, and who had so much more experience. That wasn't fair! "You should see her now!' Sharon gossiped. "She acts as if she owned the place!"

Kiki pulled Section 9 out of the Sunday Times and decided that she'd be really mature about it this time, that she'd start from scratch and not allow her hopes to get up too high. But those ads! They were so enticing! It was a constant struggle to grab her hopes and pull them back down. Some bold letters read: Int'l Affairs. She read the small print below: a top coll bkgd qualifies you for this extraordinary growth directed oppty. Dynamically growing mdtn firm seeks bilingual candidate with . . . She quickly sent them her resumé. It seemed as if she were precisely and exclusively the person they were looking for. So why didn't they call her? Why? Why? What was wrong?! "You're still aiming too high," Jamie said. "That's a 24K job! Sharon and I don't make that kind of money yet!"

At the end of March, Kiki settled for a proofreading position at Knight Meier, an enormous Wall Street law firm. The hours were 5 p.m. to 12 a.m., good hours that would allow her to spend the day looking for her dream job. And at least this was a job, her first "real" job, 15K with benefits and vacations, and dinner, and a limousine to drive her home at midnight. Was she finally getting her foot in the door? "It is a start," both Jamie and Sharon agreed. "15K!" her mother shouted. "You can make three times that amount as a maid!" At least she had a job. Somebody had actually wanted her and was paying her. She'd just keep searching for better.

She worked for a whole year at Knight Meier, and it was no fun being something other than an attorney in that gigantic building. The non-legal staff were the second-class citizens. The non-legal staff had different bathrooms and different dining rooms, the only contact with the "legals" being through their documents. The job was humiliating, and life was no fun. But Kiki would try desperately to shake herself out of this nagging depression. Wasn't she, after all, one of the privileged few? What was the grief of a twenty-six-year-old college grad who specialized in the literature of the Georgian era compared to the poverty and despair obvious everywhere in her New York City? She was just someone looking for a better job, that was all. She always had a quarter to spare, a quarter she could kindly offer to the homeless. Why was she so sad then? Was this pride? Why, why, why in the world did she chose to compare her frustrating existence to Kathryn's good luck instead of comparing it to that of the hungry, the destitute, the homeless? But it was too hard to resist. She couldn't do anything about it. That's the way it was. She was miserable. Because she not only bumped into the destitute in the subway, she also bumped into Kathryn once in a while. And Kathryn was doing so well! She was putting her knowledge of literature to good use. After having outgrown it! And Sharon was constantly complaining about Kathryn because they both worked in the same company. Except that Kathryn had her own office along with all the other things Sharon was dying to have and Jamie was dying to have and Kiki was dying to have. Why was Kathryn so lucky?

Kiki decided to have brunch with Kathryn one Saturday. A secret brunch, because Kathryn had become a persona and memoria non-grata at home. "You're wasting away, Kiki," Kathryn remarked.

"So what should I do?" Kiki asked.

"Find what's right for you," Kathryn replied.

"Oh, my God, it's him!" Kiki whispered suddenly. "It's him! It's him!"

"Who?!" Kathryn asked and turned around.

"It's him! It's him! Oh, my God, it's Kiki. This is all thanks to you, Kathryn. You're good luck. How do I look?"

"You look terrible. What do you mean it's Kiki? You're Kiki."

"But he's Kiki, too. The man I love. He saw me! Kathryn, don't turn around! He's coming over! Kathryn, pretend we're talking!"

They were in one of these brunchy restaurants on the Upper West Side of Manhattan. And Kiki was walking over to their table, and he got there at the same time as the waitress and the French toast and the eggs benedict. And the waitress was asking if they wanted something else or coffee, and Kiki suddenly stood up and said "hi!" And she told Kiki to sit down, sit down, would he like to have brunch with them? Kiki, this is my best friend, Kathryn. Kathryn this is Kiki. His real name's Enrique Cardozo.

"And how's Sara?" Kiki asked.

"Oh, so you haven't heard?" He sat down and looked around the restaurant. "I'll just sit down for a minute I'm supposed to meet someone here. Sara died about a year ago now."

"What do you mean Sara died?" Kiki asked. "Sara can't die!"

"Of breast cancer. Didn't you know she had breast cancer? That's why she was always fighting with little Sara because little Sara wanted her to have her breast removed and that would always make big Sara furious. She was convinced she could have the cancer massaged out of her system and she was seeing all these herbalists. Anyway, it failed. Oh, God. I'm making you cry on your French toast, Kiki. Kiki, sweetheart! At the end she wanted to go, you know. Here, here, hug me, come here. Come here, sweetheart."

Whoever it was that Kiki Cardozo was supposed to meet in that restaurant didn't show up. As to Kathryn, she had to meet someone at two o'clock.

"Ever been to the Museum of Natural History?" he asked.

"No," Kiki replied and started crying again.

"Come, I'll take you there. It'll cheer you up."

Kiki Xuárez stood up. He helped her put her coat on. As they walked out of the restaurant, he was saying, "I can't believe you've never been there! It's one of my favorite hangouts. Never seen the dinosaurs?" They were out on the sidewalk. It was a beautiful winter day, and this man was so gentle, and Sara was dead.

✳   ✳   ✳

This was the beginning of the happiest year of her life. And it was happy even if she knew, deep in her heart, that it wouldn't last. Up to then, her pattern had been to fall in love with other women's men. And although this man here did not belong to any particular woman at that time, he seemed to belong to all of them! He even loved every single one of them. And he mentioned names all the time as if she knew them. Evelyn. María. Ivana. Liana.

Kiki never felt any jealousy, because it just wasn't something you could feel with this strange man who seemed to belong to everyone. Besides, when she was with him, she had the impression she was the best and the first and the only one. So the other wives didn't matter. But when he first invited her to sleep over in his villa in Union City, New Jersey, Kiki did hesitate. What, with his wives there? Would they be nasty? Would there be screaming and shouting and clawing and scratching? "What, my *tías* nasty?" he asked with a wounded tone of voice. It so happened that he referred to his wives as his *tías*, his aunts. When Kiki finally decided to spend the night in that beautiful villa overlooking Manhattan, she couldn't believe her ears when he introduced her to his wives. He said, "This is *tía* Maria, this is *tía* Evelyn, this is *tía* Ivana, and *tía* Liana's out." In total, there were twelve people living in that villa: the four *tías* and the seven children, whose ages ranged from four to twenty, and Kiki Cardozo, father, "nephew," husband, provider.

No, she couldn't experience any jealousy. It would have been ridiculous. Anyway, she was too crazy about him to allow any negative feelings to interfere with her passion. The minute she saw him, she wanted him. And he treated her well, he wanted her, too, he was always available, available for everyone, could juggle several women at the same time, must have been the Moorish blood in him, he loved every single one of them and every single one of them was unique when he was with her.

"*Tía* Ivana, I love you!" he'd say as he hugged his *tía* Ivana.

Tía Ivana was the oldest of the *tías* and the mother of his twenty-year-old son, Segundo.

"Eat, child!" *tía* Ivana would say to her ex-husband or husband because she never did find out if he had divorced any of them. "Eat your soup now."

"Why don't you feed my Maiden of Orleans, too?" He'd point to Kiki and to *tía* Ivana.

"Your Maiden of Orleans doesn't like carrots, and I made her a soup without carrots," *tía* Ivana said once. "I'm warming it up for you, my child."

"What's for dinner?" *tía* María would ask.

"Rice and squid, sweetbreads, soup, milk pudding..."

"Will you make me a little steak, *tía* Ivana?" *tía* Maria would ask because she was always in the mood for something other than what was offered to her.

"Right away, child."

Before long, even Kiki Xuárez was calling Kiki Cardozo's wives "*tía*." She was even ready to be given that title one day, so long as she could be near him, and see him, and make love with him, she was eager, ready, and willing to become a *tía.* She even wondered what it took to become a *tía,* and finally rounded up the courage to ask him.

"No, you'll never become a *tía,*" he said.

"Why not? I wouldn't mind."

"Because my Maiden of Orleans hasn't blossomed yet, and if she doesn't blossom, she'll never be happy. You just need the right soil, and I don't think that soil is here."

"Kiki, can I ask you a personal question?" she asked him.

"You can try."

"What is it that you do for a living, I mean exactly?"

"I'm a mining engineer in Peru, you know that. That's why I travel so much."

"Yes, but Sara told me you have some shady business on the side."

"She said that?! God, what a bitch! Yeah, I guess I do. This villa here's worth three million, and you can't get that on a mining engineer's salary, so I smuggle. Besides, I have to support my family. Now don't rush to conclusions. I don't smuggle drugs. I'm a respectable father and husband, and I disdain anyone who smuggles drugs. I only smuggle gold."

"Oh."

Six months elapsed since Kiki quit her job at Knight Meier, and she did not work for those six months. She simply began liking herself, because he liked her and enjoyed her about as much as she did him. He treated her well. Always ready and available.

Both Sharon and Jamie were aghast, for they were post women's lib women and their "older" sisters had done all the fighting and struggling to free them, and here was their friend and roommate, Kiki, allowing a man with several wives to support her. That was no way to express gratitude to those older sisters who had so fiercely fought for her. Yes, for her. So, she wasn't supposed to let a man support her. It was a question of principle and of pride. Kiki argued that she had no pride where he was concerned. She said she was proud of that, and that even pride can be tacky at times, especially where he was concerned. She should know, she said. Still, shouldn't let a man support you. Supposed to be independent and say "I don't need you" whenever you want. Besides, Kiki, that man, was the typical bastard macho male to Jamie's and Sharon's eyes.

"But she likes him!" Ron defended Kiki with his New York accent. "Let the poor girl be. She likes him!"

"She has to do something with her life beside cater to his primitive macho needs. Who does that guy think he is?!" Sharon protested.

"So what are you going to do with your life?" Kiki's mother asked. "Just let him wrap you around his little finger? You have to stand up to him, child. Anyway, he'll soon get bored with you if you don't have a good job and an interesting life."

Her mother always knew where to strike. Perhaps she should get a job. Suddenly, she stopped loving herself like she had for the past six months and went back to the classified ads in the Sunday Times. She really had to do something with her life. Find some fantastic job with growth opportunity and prestige and travel. Maybe now, with the experience she had gotten at Knight Meier, they would take a look at her resumé and...call her? Nobody called her. Apparently she wasn't what they wanted.

A month later, she had a job as an ESL instructor on Bergenline Avenue in Union City. The commute was nothing, a mere twenty-minute walk from Kiki's villa where she was practically living without having formally moved in, for she was still paying her share of the rent for her room on Ogden Avenue.

Sometimes Kiki Cardozo would disappear for two weeks in a row, but she would remain at the villa with his children and *tías*. Kiki usually went to Ogden Avenue on Thursday nights to collect some of her things and bring some others back. Once again, she had not formally moved into the villa. Nobody had asked her to. Secretly, she was hoping that one day soon someone would offer her her own bedroom. She even hoped it would be one particular bedroom perched on the cliff and overlooking Manhattan and the Hudson River. The bedroom next to Kiki's. But nobody asked her. She simply slept in Kiki's bed, and that is why she still kept her personal belongings in the house on Ogden Avenue. So long as she didn't have her own bedroom in the villa, she had no place to put her things.

One morning in winter, he drew the blinds and the sunshine flooded the bedroom. It woke her up. The day was exceptionally clear, you could see the Empire State Building and the World Trade Center. "Good morning," she said sleepily. "I love you," she added. Then she sensed it. It was time. She knew.

"Kiki," he said. "I have to let you go."

"I know."

By noon, she had her little overnight bag packed and was kissing the *tías* good-bye. *Tía* Ivana was crying. She thought she should have lunch before leaving. But Kiki wasn't hungry. *Tía* María, too, was teary-eyed. She kept repeating, "Poor niña. Poor child!" As to the man she loved, he was still up in his bedroom, he admitted that he was too much of a coward to say good-bye, he said he was sorry, he said there were too many *tías* already, if not he would have gladly...Kiki asked him if she could at least be put on a waiting list. He said no.

* * *

1989 was a sad year for her. Her mother returned to New Jersey. Broke. And her brother fled to Costa Rica because of all the arrest warrants against him. Her sister was somewhere in Manhattan prescribing herbal remedies, pregnant, and giving massages. Kiki continued giving her classes of English as a second language every day except Friday. Friday was supposed to be her special day, and she usually went to Manhattan, either to a movie, or to a museum, or to browse in the bookstores and search for new books on Peru. Since he had left her, she'd taken a keen interest in the history of Peru. She devoured book after book about the Incas. Although he probably didn't have a drop of Inca blood in his veins, he had talked about the Incas so much that she felt closer to him just reading about them. Her favorite bookstore was Revolution Books on 17th Street. Sometimes she'd stay there all Friday afternoon leafing through the books. After the Incas, she began reading about the Aztecs. He had often talked about the Aztecs, too. He had even been the one who had told Sara about Malinche, that Aztec woman who had done all the interpreting for Cortés during the conquest of what was then called New Spain. And Sara had been so fascinated with Malinche that she had changed the name of her company to Ma-

linche. Apparently, when Moctezuma talked to Cortés he
always called him Malinche. "Are you weary, Malinche?"
Moctezuma asked. "No, I'm not weary," Cortés replied. Why
had Sara always talked to her about Malinche? "Since you
claim to be a descendant of Cortés, perhaps you should know
about Malinche," Sara once said.

"But Latin American history does not interest me," Kiki
once said. "I'm only interested in literature of the Georgian
era, that's my specialty."

"You're so *nya nya*," Sara loved to say.

He had also talked about the Maya. So after the Aztecs,
she began reading about the Maya. She read about the Maya
in Yucatan, Belize, El Salvador, Nicaragua. She then stum-
bled upon a book about the history of Jamaica, and there she
was crossing the Caribbean waters right there in Revolution
Books on 17th street, and she landed in Jamaica. Then it was
the Dominican Republic. Haiti. Puerto Rico. The Virgin
Islands. Martinique. Guadeloupe. She read all that. Sixteenth
century, seventeenth, eighteenth, nineteenth. The present.
One day, she even started to read about Cuba, what she'd
been the least interested in, her own country. She also read
about Gorbachev. She read about the Berlin Wall coming
down. She read about the Rumanians putting their tyrant to
death. She read more about Cuba. She read the classified ads
in the *New York Times*, and in the help-wanted section she
read: Once in a lifetime Offering 17K. No, no, no. No. That's
what she said. No more. She knew what she had to do now.
She had slowly been discovering the answer, right in that
bookstore. Once in a Lifetime Offering 17K. She knew what
she had to do now. It was funny, Kathryn had found out years
before. Why had it taken her this long? She had even wondered if she should proceed just like Kathryn. Of course not.
To each his own fate, his calling. But why had it taken her so
long to find out about hers? Simply because history had to
take its course. And no wonder she had had so many difficul-
ties here. Trying to force upon herself a fate that wasn't hers.
It just couldn't happen! Once in a lifetime Offering 17K. Last
time she would need the help-wanted section of the *New York
Times*. Last time.

* * *

"I can't believe Kiki actually did that," Sharon said.

"That's is the most cowardly act I've ever heard of in my whole life," Jamie added.

"Hey girls," Ron said. "So she went to live in Cuba. Maybe it's the beginning of something. Of something new, and she's simply the one who's starting it."

"Still," Sharon said. "You just don't pick up and leave for Cuba when you read an ad that says 'Once in a lifetime Offering 17K.' That's overreacting!"

"Normally, people leave their countries to find jobs here," Jamie added. "This is the land of opportunity. So what does she expect? To find a job in Cuba?"

BELLS

After having attended graduate school in California and spending half-a-year exploring the Central American countries—the other half living and working abroad—Cristina Carbone returned home to New York. She was twenty-five. Life ahead seemed as vincible as a thick textbook full of chapters and subchapters. And this suited her well, for she was methodical and organized. There was no chaos in her mind. After careful planning, everything started at step one and went on from there, carefully, steadily, intelligently. Yes, indeed, she was career-minded, but her ambition was definitely not a negative, envious one. She was curious, she liked to learn, she was busy, active, bubbling with energy, she knew no anguish, and she knew no envy, not yet.

Had she wanted, she could have made no effort at all, just waited. For one day she would inherit from her father. But thanks to her brothers' and sister's negative example, Cristina was determined to build herself a life independent of the inheritance awaiting her. She was a purist. When her father was raving mad at her siblings, he always shouted that Cristina was the "only purebred in the whole goddamn litter." At age twenty-five, having safely gotten through the "dark woods" of childhood, of adolescence, and of the early twenties that her father always ranted and raved about, it could be said, once and for all, that she hadn't let him down. But it wasn't for him that she'd been this responsible and methodical. Once again, she was a purist, she wanted to do her best, just her best. This was one of her many principles. And like most women who are preparing for a rewarding future, she had decided to postpone marriage and children. There would always be time for that.

Right away, she found a charming studio apartment on the Upper West Side, and since she didn't have a job yet, she asked her parents to help her with the security and the first month's rent. She swore she'd pay them back. They said this was out of the question. They insisted on buying her the whole building as a reward for having gotten her Master's. She said she didn't need the whole building; she wanted neighbors; she only wanted the studio apartment. So they wanted to buy her the apartment. She didn't want that either. She only wanted a small loan. She said she'd buy herself her own apartment. There was a big battle. They wondered why she wanted to go through hardships if she didn't have to. They also tried to manipulate her, to convince her that it was best to own the whole building. Cristina didn't give in. She became a tenant and even ended up painting the small apartment herself, with the help of some friends.

Immediately after having moved in, she enrolled in a part-time Ph.D. program, made fifty copies of her resumé, and began looking for a job as a journalist. A month later, in spite of her father's connections and bad reputation, she got a job as a reporter in one of the Hispanic tv stations. She soon discovered that, although her mother was Cuban and she had spoken Spanish from birth, her Spanish grammar was insufficient. So she quickly added an advanced Spanish class to her long list of activities, which also included three evenings a week at the Art Students' League. She had a gift for painting and had even earned her pocket money in California painting lampposts and wooden furniture.

By November she hardly had a minute to herself. Not only that, but she also had many friends from before she left New York and she was invited to parties at least twice a week. Often she had to turn down invitations, being either too busy or too tired to spend an evening out. Cristina knew how to organize her life and seemed in full control of all her activities, never neglecting one for the other. Life had turned out to be smooth. There were no barriers, no obstacles, no wasted time; her existence was one big rewarding effort—"this" led to "that" and "that" led to other things. It was constant, steady evolution, advancement, progress. Before she knew it, she had reached cruising altitude. How could she know envy? She wasn't standing outside looking in; she was right in the middle.

One evening, her mother told her she had gained weight and that she looked much better. For once, her father agreed with her mother and added that it was about time she stopped looking like a colt and got some flesh on her bones. "Oh, really?" Cristina asked three or four times. "You really think I've gained weight?" she inquired again and again with an increasing tone of concern in her voice.

After dinner she quickly stood up from the table and rushed to the scale in her parents' bathroom.

Indeed, she had gained almost twenty pounds. Was her metabolism changing? If at age twenty-five she had already gained twenty pounds, what would she look like at thirty? Upon reaching thirty she planned to get serious about some man and start a family. What if she was too fat? Worse yet, now that things were going so smoothly, was she going to have a weight problem? Would she have to go to Weight Watchers? Waste her time with that?! She didn't have time to be fat!

Back at the dinner table she told her parents about how worried she was. She almost weighed one hundred and forty-five pounds! "But you're five-eight! That's a good weight for a girl of five-eight!" her mother said.

Two Saturdays a month, Cristina was in the habit of dining at her parents'. Since they lived in New Jersey, and since she refused to let her father pay for a limousine to drive her back home, and since both her parents were dead set against public transportation (public being a synonym of dirty and dangerous), Cristina usually ended up spending the night there. In bed that night she thought that it was normal that she had gained weight, for she spent, after all, half her lifetime sitting down, and the only exercise she got was running from the subway to the bus to the subway to the office and then back home. What else could she expect? In fact, she had been so busy lately that she had forgotten not only to include some kind of physical exercise in her long list of activities, but also to take a good look at herself.

On Sunday afternoon, after careful deliberation, Cristina decided to take up the elbow-locking, teeth-clenching Japanese martial art of Jujitsu instead of modern dance, or tennis or jogging, or simple calisthenics. According to her plans, Jujitsu should fulfill the triple function of making her stay in shape, protecting her in New York City, and, last but not least, allowing her to meet men. Yes, indeed, in the past few weeks Cristina had begun to be concerned. The man she was in love with and had left behind in California was no longer writing to her. Or perhaps she was just lending too much of an ear to what her girlfriends said about New York City not being the place to meet men. At first Cristina merely laughed at their whining complaints, but in late November she began to wonder. Perhaps they were right. She counted six months since she'd arrived in New York. Many parties, many dinners, but she always returned home alone. Because she was still in love? But she hadn't heard from him in such a long time! This wasn't really paving the way for her thirtieth birthday when she was supposed to meet the man of her life and marry him. So she became more receptive to her girlfriends' painful chit-chat. At parties, when they danced with each other or bor-rowed, for a three-minute dance, either somebody's boyfriend or a married man, as if these men were nice shoes or shirts, they wondered where in the world to get them. At work? No. Because you're supposed to be professional, and if it doesn't work out you're stuck from nine-to-five with somebody you hate. In a bar? No way! And certainly not in a modern-dance class. As to tennis courts, Cristina's available girlfriends had already tried. They always ended up playing a boring game with other available beginner girls while the eligible men con-centrated three courts away on their own game. Sometimes they even brought girls with them. They concluded and agreed that striving to meet a man at a tennis court equaled wanting to marry a doctor when you're a nurse. Too late, they're already taken.

In truth, Cristina was in no big hurry. She just liked to look ahead, get an early start on her thirtieth birthday. Nev-ertheless, her thirtieth birthday remained five years away. Moreover, she had her career to think about, and her Ph.D., and her advanced Spanish classes, and her art, and her friends, and her parents, and this absent man who wasn't writing to her. She loved spending hours thinking about him, so how could she squeeze a new man amongst all that? There was neither the time in her agenda nor a place in her mind.

The minute she stepped on the mat for her first Jujitsu class she changed her mind.

His name was Fujiwara. He was the instructor. A sev-enth dan Black Belt, and apparently that was high. And although he wasn't quite as tall as she was, he was well-built and handsome, with long black hair and a bushy beard because he was from Northern Japan. The men from the south didn't have as much hair as the northern ones, this she overheard in the dressing room the first night. She also asked how old he was, just out of curiosity. And he turned out to be forty-eight. That meant that he was twenty-three years older than she. Forty-eight, she said to herself. He'd probably think she was just a baby.

Fujiwara didn't speak English very well, and he spoke so softly that you could barely hear what he was saying. And although Cristina could only attend classes once a week, she did make rapid progress in this martial art. Three months later, she was taking her first test, and for a beginner she succeeded so well with all the techniques that Fujiwara finally noticed her.

That evening the Jujitsu students went with their instructor to a bar in Tribeca to celebrate. Cristina found a way to sit next to Fujiwara, who began asking her many questions. He wanted to know what she did, where she lived, where she was originally from, and he seemed quite interested in all her answers. It must be very interesting to be a journalist, he commented. And did she travel very much? She told him of her trips to Nicaragua and Honduras and Uruguay. She said it had all happened very quickly. At first she was hired as a cub reporter, but a month later they decided they liked her so much that they promoted her, and now they were even sending her on special assignments. And the Upper West Side was a very pleasant place to live, wasn't it? Oh, Cristina said she loved it but didn't really have the time to enjoy or explore her neighborhood. On the weekends, she was either working on her Ph.D. or traveling. Not to mention the art classes that she could only attend once a week now, her job being so demanding. And the Jujitsu, of course, which she loved. She was even going to try to come twice a week from now on. And where had she learned Spanish? Oh, that was easy. Her mother was Cuban and her father was half-Mexican and half-Italian, which explained why her last name was Italian. Fujiwara said that was a very interesting combination, Cuban and Italian, and he also said he loved the Spanish language and would love to learn it one day. "Oh, I'll teach you," Cristina volunteered.

From there on, it was all uphill. Fujiwara was such a gentle man. He spoke softly and kissed her tenderly and meditated for hours. Cristina was greatly impressed by him, he was so wise and relaxed and such a master of his art. She admired real vocations. She also felt bad that he lived in such a tiny, roach-infested apartment in Tribeca. He didn't even have sunlight! She wondered what he ate when she wasn't around. She began worrying about him. Did he have enough money? How could she be of help? Should she ask him to move in with her and stop worrying about such prosaic things as electricity and rent? Why keep that stinky place in Tribeca anyway? Wasn't he staying at her place every single night? Even when she was away he slept there.

"So tell me about him," Cristina's cousin Sylvia said one night on the phone when Fujiwara was away in London for a week giving a Jujitsu and meditation seminar.

"Oh, he's fantastic, Sylvia. If you only knew. He is so intelligent and spiritual that it's really overwhelming. I feel tiny next to him. God, I admire him so much!"

"Spiritual, intelligent . . . What about the rest?" Sylvia inquired.

"It's simple. I am head over heels in love with him! I've even signed up for a Japanese class. You never know, we'll probably end up living in Japan one of these days."

"This really sounds serious, Cris!"

"Please don't call me Cris. Well, anyway, I'll be twenty-six next month, and he's forty-eight...You know what I mean? I mean we're not going to rush into anything...or anything like that...You know what I mean? I mean I've been more or less trying to get my parents ready for this, you know what I mean?"

"By the way, I saw you on tv the other day. I'm so proud of you! Too bad it's Hispanic tv...but I guess you can't have everything!"

"Sylvia! What do you mean 'too bad it's Hispanic tv'? You should be ashamed! You're Hispanic yourself! Anyway, our news crew is worth any news crew in the world. I even think we're better!"

On the day of Fujiwara's return from London, Cristina went to greet him at the airport with a special surprise, a stretch luxury limousine to drive them home. Fujiwara seemed embarrassed. He told Cristina she shouldn't have, they could've taken the J.F.K. Express back. "The J.F.K. Express! Are you kidding?!" Cristina exclaimed. "You deserve no more and no less than a limousine!"

The driver opened the door and asked them to step in please. There was even a bar back there, and Cristina had arranged to have a bottle of chilled Champagne waiting for Fujiwara. "This is the best and the most expensive Champagne in the world!" she said as she handed him the bottle. Fujiwara had never opened a bottle of Champagne. "Here I'll do it," Cristina said. "Sixty-eight dollars a bottle," she added. "And it's delicious, you'll see. You'll love it, Fujiwara." Fujiwara preferred to drink tomato juice. Cristina told him it was out of the question, he absolutely had to drink the Champagne, so he reluctantly sipped the sixty-eight-dollar Champagne and thanked her.

He then said he preferred to go and spend the night in his studio in Tribeca. The trip had tired him, and he wanted to relax and meditate. But Cristina wouldn't have it. She had reserved at La Côte Basque restaurant. Was he going to turn La Côte Basque down for his stupid little alfalfa pills and bee pollen and grimy little studio in Tribeca? Oh, and speaking of that disgusting little place, shouldn't he move out of it? "It's absolutely ridiculous to hang on to it," Cristina said. "It's such a gloomy place!" she added. "Oh, I love you so much, Fujiwara!" she exclaimed, throwing her arms around him and loudly kissing his cheeks and forehead.

"By the way, my tv station's going to have a BIG, and I mean BIG, party on the twenty-third," Cristina mentioned when they were finally seated at La Côte Basque restaurant.

They'd changed tables three times already, the first table having been too close to the door, the second one too close to the kitchen, and the third one just not good enough. Cristina had even raised her voice. Nothing would do! She wondered, out loud, if this restaurant was any good. She wanted the best, goddammit. She was paying! It was their responsibility to give her a good table! A shy, embarrassed Fujiwara had tried to convince her that any table would do, but she wouldn't have it. She wasn't going to let a couple of stupid waiters order her around! They finally settled for the fourth table, although it wasn't exactly what she had expected. She mumbled and grumbled a little more, but ten minutes later this whole incident was forgotten. There were other things to talk about. She wasn't going to let her evening be ruined, no she wasn't! "So, I ordered a suit for you at Bergdorf's so you could accompany me to the party," she told Fujiwara. "Shit, I didn't bring my appointment book! I don't know if I scheduled you for a fitting tomorrow or the day after. Remind me to tell you tonight, O.K.? It's really important. Anybody who's anybody in the Hispanic world will be there."

Fujiwara timidly suggested that perhaps Cristina should go by herself. He said he didn't fit in that kind of party because he didn't speak English very well, much less Spanish. But just when he was about to give a third reason for not going, Cristina interrupted him. He absolutely had to go with her! Even her father would be there! And it was about time he met her father. "Oh, I'm so crazy about you, Fujiwara!" she exclaimed. "You are the handsomest, most intelligent, and most spiritual man in the world! I'm so proud of you! I love you! I love you! I love you!"

Fujiwara smiled. He was embarrassed.

That night Cristina wanted to make love and Fujiwara wanted to meditate. "Tomorrow you'll have the whole day to meditate!" she told him. "While I'm at work," she added. "But don't forget to go to Bergdorf's to get your suit fitted! Don't you forget!"

It so happened that Fujiwara had a Jujitsu seminar in Philadelphia scheduled for the twenty-third. Cristina took the liberty of canceling it. He absolutely had to go to the party with her. He'd promised. Fujiwara was a bit perplexed. They never quarreled though. Fujiwara seemed to take things as they came.

Everything went smoothly at the party until Fujiwara told Cristina's father that he was a Jujitsu instructor and Cristina's father asked, "Whawhawhahat kind of job is that?!" Fujiwara had then expatiated on the subject, thinking that Cristina's father wanted to know more. "Sounds like a lot of goddamn rubbish to me!" Cristina's father said and walked away.

Fujiwara had a seminar in Chicago the week after, so Cristina took a few days off from work because she wanted to surprise him when he got back. The surprise was a loft she had bought in Chelsea for both of them. In secret, she had written to Fujiwara's landlord to announce he was moving out, and she actually moved him out of there in the few days he was away. Their new home was beautiful. She had even provided Fujiwara with a meditation room so he could meditate while she was traveling or at work.

* * *

"Sorry to hear about your med schools," Cristina told her cousin Sylvia on the phone. Her voice was sad.

"Well, I have no choice but to go and study in Santo Domingo," Sylvia replied. "If no med school wants me here, tough! I'm so bitter, I swear. But I'll become a doctor whether they want me or not."

"But I hear those Dominican diplomas are worthless," Cristina said.

"Once I finish my internship there I'll just come back here and take a test," Sylvia said. "So did you two really split up?" she asked.

"Yeah," Cristina replied, her voice sad. "It's too bad. Fujiwara was really a fantastic man. Still is. My fault, you know. All of a sudden I started acting like my father...bossing him around, telling him what to do, what not to do. I can't believe it. I was madly in love with him and became a monster in order to prove it. And I did everything wrong. Well, if there's ever a next time...I swear I won't make the same mistakes if there's ever a next time. Now I'm trying to turn this into a positive experience, you know what I mean? If I don't...I think I'll die...oh, I'm crying again! I just can't stop!"

"Cheer up, Cristina!" Sylvia said. "What's one mistake?!" she asked after what seemed like a minute of sorrowful silence. "You're only twenty-six!" she nervously added.

Cristina didn't quit Jujitsu though. She wasn't one to quit anything she'd begun. Moreover, she had another Jujitsu test coming up. And Fujiwara was an excellent instructor. They became good friends. Shortly after they separated, Fujiwara started seeing Laura, another one of his students. And even Laura and Cristina became good friends.

But she did have to quit going to the Art Students' League. Work was very demanding, and she was traveling to South America once every two weeks. She also had her Ph.D. and her Japanese classes and her Jujitsu test. She was a broken-hearted, busy girl.

* * *

Mark was one of Fujiwara's Black Belts. Cristina had known him for over a year now. She thought he was "sweet" and funny. They liked to joke around in class. He used to love kidding her about being "taller than Fujiwara." Then after Cristina and Fujiwara separated, and in order to cheer her up, he began kidding her about being "tall...that's all. Just plain tall." He also called her "gorgeous" and loved repeating that, if he weren't in love with his ex-wife, he'd be in love with her.

A native New Yorker, Mark had spent many years living and working in Japan as an investment banker. He had even married a Japanese woman who had given him three lovely daughters. "She was a perfect woman in Japan," he liked saying. "Then we moved here four years ago," he told and retold her, "because a Japanese company offered me a good job. Boy, did she become assertive here in New York!"

Although Mark worked hard and traveled frequently, he came to Jujitsu class as often as possible because it was the only way, he said, to relieve stress. When he became serious, he also added that Jujitsu was the only pleasure he had in his life now that his wife had left him and he had no family life. He missed his three daughters whom he only got to see twice a month. His Japanese wife had remarried and was still living in New York. Mark was extremely jealous of the new husband, not so much because of his wife, he swore, but because of his three daughters.

He began helping Cristina prepare for her next test. They soon discovered they had very much in common. After class, they took to going to the bar around the corner and speaking Japanese together. He was fluent, and Cristina was getting the chance of a lifetime to practice this language. They were also very busy people. They often took the same cab to Kennedy Airport together. When he was flying to Singapore, she was on her way to Peru or Costa Rica.

"I guess you won't be needing me anymore!" Mark said to Cristina the day she passed her test.

"Are you kidding?!" exclaimed Cristina. "I need you more than ever! Let's go to the bar so I can practice my Japanese and celebrate."

"Very good test," Fujiwara walked up to her and said.

"Oh, thank you, Fujiwara!" Cristina exclaimed, embracing him. "Oh, Laura, I love your outfit!" she turned and said to Laura.

At the bar, after having joked for a while, Mark suddenly got serious and said, "I guess you're not over him yet."

"You know what?" Cristina replied. "I think I am. It was just a question of forgiving myself for having turned into such a monster in that relationship. I know better now."

"I know what you mean," Mark commented. "I guess I messed things up with my wife. Now here I am! Living without my daughters!"

"Mark, I would absolutely love to meet your daughters one of these days. I bet they're lovely!"

"That they are!" Mark replied.

First they talked about his daughters' ages. The youngest was nine, the oldest was fifteen. "Fifteen!" exclaimed Cristina. "How old does that make you then?"

"It'll be the big four-o pretty soon," he answered.

Yes, it was incredible. Forty, and so soon. Life had just begun. He'd barely seen the years pass. They both had the impression the years were getting shorter and shorter. Cristina, in turn, said she couldn't believe she'd be twenty-seven in two months. That's when they began comparing their respective ages. He was thirteen years older than she. "You're just a baby," he said.

"Sure!" she said. "A baby who's almost middle-aged."

"I think you're too young for me," Mark kidded her in Japanese.

"Yeah! You'd be robbing the cradle!" Cristina joked.

"Talking about robbing the cradle..." Mark remembered. "When I first met my wife, she was seventeen and I was twenty-two, and everybody kept repeating that she was a baby. Now she's thirty-five! Somehow we never think we're going to get old...When I married her, I thought I'd always have a little girl for a wife. Now she's thirty-five!"

"And she's not your wife."

They began having dinner together whenever they weren't traveling. Cristina was an excellent cook, and Mark was getting tired of his divorced man's beer-and-mixed-nuts dinners. Her loft became a haven for him. He liked everything about it. Even the smell of it. He also loved her bed. He said it was the most comfortable bed he'd ever slept in. As for Cristina, at first she thought his nostrils were too big and she didn't like his feet either. They were flat and his big toes were ridiculously big; they almost sat over on the other toes. And there was a big bone on the side of each foot, sticking out. But Mark began worshipping the ground Cristina walked on. When they were making love, he repeated he'd never met a woman like her before. He even talked about wanting to have a child with her. She still thought she was too young.

One Monday afternoon, Mark was supposed to fly to London, spend two days taking care of his company's business in London, and then fly to Hong Kong where he was to stay a whole week. Cristina accompanied him to Kennedy Airport, and on their way there, he kept repeating that ten days was too long a time to spend without her. A little later, while standing in line, he just couldn't stop hugging and kissing her and telling her he loved her more than anything in the world. When it was Mark's turn to show his ticket and passport and check his luggage in, the British Airways employee asked if they'd be two traveling. "Yes, the two of us here," Mark replied. When Cristina told the British Airways employee that Mark was just kidding, Mark said he was dead serious. He even had a ticket for her and her passport and a toothbrush, "see!"

"Mark, I can't just leave like that!" Cristina argued.

"When's the last time you had a vacation, Cristina?"

"I've never had a vacation. I don't believe in vacations. My father convinced me a long time ago that vacations are for the dying and the ill. Anyway, I can't pick up and go! I have my job!"

After Cristina had repeated "I can't go" several times and Mark had insisted "Yes, you can" several other times, Cristina gave in. She had to make several phone calls though. She thought this was crazy. She said, "this is really crazy!" She had no time for a vacation!

"Mark, this is really crazy," she said, once they were seated in the plane.

"This is the craziest thing I've ever done in my life," she commented when a cab was driving them to their hotel in London.

She kept calling her tv station, asking if everything was going smoothly without her. Was everything under control? Would they call her the minute anything went wrong? She gave orders and more orders, and always left a number where she could be reached. She worried. She pulled her hair. She imagined all sorts of catastrophes. In Hong Kong she warned

Mark that if anything happened in South America she'd just have to pick up and go. He said, "Relax! You deserve a vacation. And I love you."

Back in New York, Cristina barely had the time to realize how much she'd enjoyed this trip to London and Hong Kong. It was work, work, work, then flying to Miami for a day, then to El Salvador, spending two days in El Salvador, flying back to New York, one day in New York, a bad night's sleep, a hectic morning at the station, then rushing back home to pick up her suitcase and her passport, rushing to Kennedy Airport, rushing to Bogota, Colombia, to interview someone. This is how a whole month went by. She then had a quiet weekend. Saturday was spent working on her Ph.D., followed by a nice quiet dinner with Mark at home that same evening. On Sunday she accompanied Mark and his three daughters to the Museum of Modern Art and a movie.

At first Cristina liked those three girls. She thought they were charming. And "cute" was the word she used to describe the way Mark behaved with them. "He acts as if they were porcelain dolls!" she told her cousin Sylvia Bos on the phone. "Never seen anything as cute in my life! How's the Dominican Republic?"

Eight months into their relationship, she was used to comforting Mark on those depressing Sunday evenings after he had dropped his precious daughters off at their mother's. Sometimes he even wept, and Cristina would rub his neck and be gentle and understanding. But something happened on that particular Sunday afternoon at the Museum of Modern Art. It wasn't anything the girls did, they were as charming, as pretty, and as Japanese as ever. But suddenly Mark's fatherly alacrity irritated her. Suddenly she hated Mark. Suddenly she hated his girls. And his ex-wife. And his past. All those years he had spent without loving her. Suddenly she felt a deep, painful pang of jealousy.

And it didn't go away. It just intensified. Cristina became moody. She said she was tired. Wanted to go home. Took a cab. Stupid Mark with his big nostrils stayed behind. The cab pulled out and he was standing there on the sidewalk, waving bye-bye. And his three daughters, too, were waving bye-bye.

That evening, instead of getting his routine shoulder to cry on, and back rub, and hugs and kisses, and tenderness, and lips drying his fatherly tears and repeating that they understood him, he heard, "Go fucking cry elsewhere! I'm getting sick and tired of your fucking Sunday-evening weeping!"

They didn't talk to each other for three days. But they made up on Thursday. Cristina begged for his forgiveness. She said she didn't know what had gotten over her. She blamed her outburst on being tired, overworked, and too busy. Mark said it was all his fault. He was ready to start crying all over again, this time for a different reason. He was so ashamed! How could he have been so selfish! He hated himself for not having paid enough attention to her! They had a delightful evening. Cristina felt that Mark was all hers. She was happy.

But the jealousy didn't go away. It got worse. Like mildew, it continued spreading over her heart each day. Often, before a Jujitsu class, Cristina would go and meet Mark at his place then tell him to go on ahead by himself. She'd stay in his apartment and wait for him. The minute he was gone and she heard the elevator doors shut, she'd start going through his closets and drawers and big cardboard boxes with a fine-tooth comb, searching for letters, photos, traces of his marriage that would gnaw at her frantic heart. One by one, she ripped all the photos of his ex-wife and burned her letters and even got rid of odds and ends Mark had brought back from Japan after having lived there for so many years. She also stopped wanting to practice her Japanese with him. For a few months, her sole aim was to eliminate anything that was Japanese from his memory and his heart. The next time he had to pick his daughters up at their mother's, she pretended to be terribly ill. The time after that, she heated up a thermometer and told him she had a fever. Couldn't he cancel, please? He could see his daughters in two weeks.

Two weeks later she put her index finger down her throat and threw up. What was wrong? Mark canceled again. He hadn't seen his daughters for over a month. Then she ran out of hysterical illnesses. But she never wanted him to see his daughters again. In a fit of rage, she ripped all of their pictures in front of him.

She spent her twenty-eighth birthday alone, on a special assignment in the Dominican Republic. At least her cousin Sylvia Bos was there, and they had dinner together.

"Sorry to hear about you and Mark splitting up," Sylvia said.

"Oh, I'm so ashamed of myself! Don't talk about it, Sylvia, please! Let's just eat."

"So what can we talk about?" Sylvia asked.

"I get so weird when I fall in love," Cristina said. "Everything was going extremely well with Mark until the minute I fell in love with him! Then I turned into a monster! But let's not talk about that. How is distance treating you and Carlos?"

"Promise not to tell your mother?" Sylvia whispered.

"Oh, my God, another Bos family secret! You people must have the 'let's keep it a secret' syndrome. And you invent these incredible stories in order to hide the normal things that happen to you. Like that time your mother thought she was too old to be pregnant. I'll never forget that! Anyway, what is it now?"

"Carlos and I divorced," Sylvia whispered.

"Really? I mean you're telling me the truth, aren't you? It's not in order to keep everyone from finding out that Carlos has a broken arm or something like that..."

"Cross my heart."

"Oh, my God!" exclaimed Cristina. "Twenty-three years old and you're already divorced! Well, I can understand, you're absolutely gorgeous, I've never seen anybody as cute as you...Oh, my God! I can't believe this! And you're only twenty-three! So what is it now?"

"I got tired of him," Sylvia shrugged. "The exact same way I got tired of, you know, that guy Antonio, whom I was engaged to. It's easy. I can't stay with a man for more than six months. It's like clockwork, on our six-month anniversary I'm not in love anymore. But don't tell your mother because she'll tell my mother and my mother'll kill me because she doesn't want anyone to know. She's going to pretend I'm still married for the next two years. Of course, she's not even telling anyone that I'm planning to marry someone else now."

"You are so lucky!" exclaimed Cristina.

"I don't know about that. Look at your career and look at mine. I got so distracted with my marriage that no med school in the U.S. wanted me. And look at where I'm studying medicine now! And I'm in love again, so even here I'm flunking out."

"Yeah, but...God, Carlos was so handsome!"

"I know, but the new one's even handsomer. Oh, by the way, Carlos studies Jujitsu in your school. I guess you've never run across him..."

"No! God, I'd love to see him! He must go to morning class...I should go to morning class one of these days and see what he's up to."

"He's just a beginner," Sylvia said.

"Well, I'm just a second kyu."

"A lot that means to me."

"That means I have one more test before my Black-Belt test."

"You're so modest, Cristina. What about your Ph.D.?"

"That's for June."

*　*　*

Carlos was thirty-four. When Cristina finally ran across him at a morning Jujitsu class, he had been divorced for nearly nine months. And he had returned to Elizabeth, New Jersey, to live with his mother. His father had died when he was a child, and he was an only child. It was only during those short months of marriage to Sylvia Bos that he had lived away from his mother. And he went back to her the minute Sylvia left him. His mother was a strong, courageous woman who, without speaking a word of English and all by herself, had managed to put her son through school, college, and graduate school. Carlos had become a relatively successful engineer, and his mother was very proud of him.

"Hey! How are you?!" Carlos said the first time he ran across Cristina at Jujitsu.

Immediately, he was impressed by her skills in this art, and he was equally impressed because she was much more advanced than he, and because he often saw her on tv. "Oh, so you watch Spanish tv?" Cristina asked.

"My mother does," Carlos replied. "We watch the news while we're having dinner. So I always see you. Hey, that's really great! You must have a spectacular life! I bet you travel a lot."

"Well, yes. I'm a reporter, I have to."

At first Cristina thought he was a bit "tacky." He appeared so naive! She thought of him as a corn-fed boy raised in New Jersey who'd traveled as far as New York

City...And he wasn't very discreet either. He even dared ask her how much money she made, just like that, out of the blue, five minutes after their first encounter in class. "What is it to you?" Cristina asked jokingly, not wanting to offend him. But he didn't get it. He even insisted. So she finally told him. And while he was saying that she made more money than he did, Cristina was thinking that he was probably the most vulgar person she'd ever met.

"Do you want to go and have a drink with me or something?" Carlos asked.

And she replied, "Some other time."

He then said, "Hey, why don't you give me your phone number or something?"

She told him she was never at home. And she didn't see him for two weeks. Then one morning he called her at the station and said, "Hey! If you don't go to Jujitsu class, I'll probably end up having a higher rank than you soon."

She explained that she went to evening class. So he asked, "Hey! Do you want us to go out or something like that?"

She said she really didn't have the time, but not wanting to offend him, she promised to have a drink with him "one of these days...soon." She said she'd call him, that too she promised. Another two weeks elapsed. So he called her back and said, "Hey! You didn't call me or anything!" She explained that she was too busy. So he began going to evening class.

Since Cristina thought she couldn't stand him, she changed her schedule. Now, she took the afternoon class during her lunch hour. Somehow he found out about that. Before long, he was sending love letters and jewelry and candies to her tv station. Cristina said, "leave me alone!" So he decided to send roses. A dozen ruby-red roses arrived each day at her station. By Friday her office looked like a hospital room. The following week the dozen roses became two dozen roses, so Cristina began distributing roses to the secretaries and her co-workers. Suddenly the newsroom looked like a greenhouse, and Carlos became the laughingstock of the tv station. Thanks to him almost everyone had roses on their desks. They even knew about him at the switchboard where there were constantly two dozen red roses in a vase. People who visited the station commented about how everyone at WGHB seemed to have a taste for red roses.

And the love letters continued pouring in. He wrote about how much he loved Cristina because she was so mysterious. Once he even wrote, "Cristina, I love you," on what seemed like one-thousand index cards and dumped these all along 24th street, where she lived. There were index cards scattered from Sixth to Seventh Avenue. He'd done that before dawn, knowing that, when she wasn't traveling, she stepped out of her building at six a.m. in order to get an early start at work.

"I'm going to call the police!" Cristina threatened him.

That same evening he spent the whole night in her elevator, hysterically ringing her doorbell. At five a.m. she let him in and offered him toast and coffee. She noticed that he smelled good and that he was handsome. He said he idolized her. He asked her what she wanted. His blood? His life? He swore that up to now women had been nothing to him, just disposable objects, but that she was like Paradise. He even compared her in beauty and goodness and mystery to the Beatrice of Dante.

"Are you sure you're in your right mind?" Cristina asked.

"I want you to be the mother of my children!" he replied.

He caught her at a time when she was weary and tired. She'd gotten her Ph.D. in June. Work was as hectic as ever. Life was one big rush. Sometimes she'd stay in the office until three in the morning, then rush home, try to get two hours sleep, pack her bags, cover the circles under her eyes with makeup, jump on an airplane. Was it all worthwhile? Those rare times that she looked at herself closely in a mirror, she noticed lines around her lips and eyes. Was she getting old or was she simply tired? She was almost twenty-nine. In fourteen months she'd be thirty. Then thirty-one. Thirty-two. Thirty-three. Then what? More money? More success? No man?

She looked down at his legs, his thighs. Full of life. And he smelled good. And his hair was thick and brown. She wanted to touch it. Was it silky? Was it soft? Fujiwara had married Laura. Mark was living with a Filipino girl. How long had it been now?

A month later she was cooking dinner for Carlos and ironing his shirts and his pants. He liked a perfect pleat that went all the way down. He usually spent the night at her place when she wasn't traveling. His mother took to calling in the morning and asking if he planned to spend another night out. There was usually an argument. Cristina often heard him say, "Mom, please don't cry."

"She's afraid you'll take me away from her," Carlos explained.

Cristina didn't think much of it. This just proved how attached he was to his mother. This probably meant he was a good person and would respect her, as much as he respected his mother, always. But shouldn't he move out of her place? Shouldn't they live together? Weren't they planning to get married and have a baby?

Cristina started wanting this more than anything. So she cooked and ironed more and more, just so Carlos would feel that he didn't need his mother that much. She never did get around to meeting his mother though. She hadn't even seen her at the wedding when Carlos had married Sylvia because his mother was angry then and had refused to attend. No, Cristina never got around to meeting her. And the way things stood, a friendly meeting was getting all the more unlikely every day. Carlos was spending more and more time in her loft because he said he loved her loft and felt "really good" there. And his mother was calling more and more often. Things even got out of hand. One morning, his mother called and told Cristina she was nothing but a whore. Cristina took the insult calmly and with serenity. She handed Carlos the receiver and told him what his mother had just said.

Instead of defending her, Carlos took the receiver, listened quietly for what seemed like an hour, then started repeating, "Mom, don't cry, please! Don't cry! You know I love you." So Cristina got angry. After he hung up, she confronted him. She said something like "it's either your mother or me!"

No woman could compete with his mother, so it seemed. Carlos packed his things and left that very same morning. He said that it was really too bad, because he loved her loft, if she ever wanted to sell it at a good price...His last words were, "You'd lost your mystery anyway."

*　*　*

When she turned thirty, men suddenly started becoming her age. There was Aaron, for example, who was only four months older. Aaron was about as big a mistake as Carlos. Aaron the artist, because she was back at the Art Students' League two evenings a week. Upon completion of her Ph.D., she had found a little empty space that needed filling. So it was the Art Students' League.

Aaron had been going there for ten years. He took as many classes as he could, which left him with little or no time to do his own work, to be creative, or so he said. He often skipped classes though, because he overslept. Sometimes he slept until two in the afternoon. It wasn't wasted time though, he often dreamt of the paintings he would paint one day, as soon as he had the time and the energy. He didn't need to earn a living anyway. His parents had left him insurance money when they died in an auto accident.

Aaron was Costa Rican, but he was born in New York City and his parents had wanted to give him what they considered to be an American name. Aaron Rodríguez. Aaron the artist. Aaron the drug-addict. She never even suspected it. He just seemed mellow, and she was glad of that. Besides, she was too busy trying to be the perfect woman at that time. She was too busy controlling her bossy, jealous, and gullible side.

"I will not be bossy," she told herself whenever she felt like giving Aaron an order. "I will not tell him that perhaps he should stop sleeping until three p.m. That's being bossy." And she wasn't jealous either. Theirs was an open relationship. Often, he wouldn't come home for dinner. So she thought there had probably been a misunderstanding. He was probably convinced she was traveling. She'd spend hours and hours controlling her feelings, her volcanic side. And when he finally got home at two or three in the morning, she simply asked him if there had been a misunderstanding and if he had eaten dinner.

"Babe, I thought you were away!" he'd say. And of course he hadn't had dinner. His life was chaos when he thought she was away.

"Aaron, you can't go to bed on an empty stomach!" Cristina would say. So she'd reheat the special dinner she had prepared seven hours before especially for him. Aaron the artist. Aaron the drug-addict.

She found out that night when the police called her. He'd been arrested. She threw a coat on, hopped into a cab, and went to post bail for him. There was a very young girl with long blond hair already there. The minute she saw Cristina she got up and said, "Oh! You must be Cristina! Aaron has told me so much about you! He says you're like a mother to him! Can you? Can you post bail for him?" Of course she could. What was money for? It was to help people. She was such a good Mommy with it. Aaron Rodríguez. Two wasted years.

Then her youngest brother died. Cristina decided to take two weeks off from work to comfort her mother who had a nervous breakdown. The next few months were mainly spent with her parents. They needed her. She was like a mother to them. She didn't learn. She thought being a Mommy was the answer. There were so many people who needed her. She thought that was the only way. To pay them back in kind for saying they loved her.

Having gotten over her brother's death, she began to think of men again. How old was she? Thirty-two going on thirty-three. There wasn't that much time left! What had gone wrong? She began comparing herself with other women. Was this one here pretty? How old was she? And already been married once. Who cared if she was divorced. She had at least a ten-point lead.

Her cousin Sylvia Bos, for example, was rushing into her third marriage, and she wasn't even thirty yet. Three marriages! Three men who went as far as to marry her! Why was it so easy for her? When Cristina wasn't working or painting or practicing Jujitsu, she was being eaten alive by envy. It was like an infection. She tried filling up every single minute of her waking life, in vain. There was always that split second. How old is that woman? Has she already been married? And had she had children before the high-risk time?

But she was convinced she'd found the solution to all her problems. Being a Mommy. They can't leave you if they depend on you. Perhaps it hadn't worked out with Aaron. But that was because he was in love with somebody else. And he never said anything about it. Just kept it to himself. A secret. A lie. But it was bound to work with the next man. She'd practiced. She was good at it now! The next one! It had to be the next one! It absolutely had to . . . whoever he was. She'd failed one too many times. How old was she now? Thirty-four? Already?! "I'm running out of time," she thought. She had a terrible fight with her father, and she even convinced herself that now that she was rid of his tyrannical presence she'd find a man. It had been her father's fault all this time. The bossy, nagging, exuberant presence of her father all these years had most likely been holding her back.

Now that she was emotionally free from her father, she'd better hurry. Men were getting younger every day. They were getting younger by the hour, the minute, the second. Angel was only twenty-nine. He was fresh from Cuba. A poet-journalist fresh from Cuba. That's what she had needed all her life, a poet-journalist! And he spoke more Russian than English, which made him exotic. And he was a very good poet. Most of all, he needed her. She hired him as her assistant.

That didn't exactly work out. She heard herself saying, "Shit, Angel, what kind of shit work is this?" Hadn't she told him a thousand times how to do this? Was he stupid? And who was he to disobey an order she gave him?! She even threatened to fire him. When he wanted to relax, she ordered him to write poetry. She certainly wasn't gong to repeat Aaron. She threatened to fire him again. A lazy bum, that's what he was. Never should've hired him. She didn't really mean it, but her job was a high-pressure job. She was used to yelling at her assistants. But Angel thought she meant it. The result was that he fled back to Castrist Cuba.

This only exacerbated Cristina's impatience. She became so uptight that men couldn't tolerate her for more than seven days now. It was failure, after failure, after failure. She even began looking over her shoulder for fear that people were laughing at her behind her back. Probably asking themselves how old she was. And never been married? Nobody wants her? Can't find a man? Poor girl, what has she done with her life? What a failure. She had failure written all over her face. Too late now. She'll never get anywhere.

The earth moved under San Francisco. Cristina went there. But she didn't care. What mattered was that men were getting younger by the hour, the minute, the second. How old is Frederick-Charles? Yes, Frederick-Charles, the photographer over there. The one taking pictures of the bridge that collapsed. Twenty-six? "Oh, my God!" Cristina thought. "Ten years younger than me!"

There were no prologues with Frederick-Charles. Not even a preliminary conversation about what she did and where she lived. No love letters. No blazing declarations. The second time she saw him, she barely had the time to ask him where he had gotten his British accent. They were in Romania. She heard him tell someone he was originally from Jamaica. So she joined the conversation and asked him why he spoke like an Englishman. "I was raised in London for a while," he replied. Clic clic clic clic went his camera. There wasn't even that moment when you wonder if it's really going to happen. They were in Romania. He said he was originally from Jamaica, raised in London. They were in bed an hour later. She didn't even have the time to decide what she should be like. Mysterious? Motherly? Cheery? Blasé? Distant? He then said, "See you around!" And she thought she'd never see him again, that she wouldn't have to choose between five or six possible behavior patterns. But that same evening, he knocked at her hotel-room door, and when she opened it, he didn't even greet her, he just said politely that he had taken quite a liking to it.

The hotel must have been close to a cathedral, for she could hear bells every fifteen minutes. At midnight, they rang twelve times. Frederick-Charles sat up and said, "hear those bells."

She wondered if that was a question, so she ventured to say, "Of course I hear those bells." He then said, as if it were a confession, that he was "into bells."

"Especially Tibetan bells," he added. "But actually any bell will do. I love all bells." Since she didn't quite know what to say and felt compelled to act interested, or say something, anything, so he wouldn't think she was a bore, she asked him if he liked bells as objects or for the sound they made. "Both, actually," he replied. "I don't like them, I love them," he corrected her.

"So how does a Jamaican photographer raised in London fall in love with Tibetan bells?" Cristina asked Frederick-Charles when they were on the plane and she had managed to get a seat next to him.

"The same way a Cuban-Italian-Mexican-American becomes a Black Belt in a Japanese martial art," he replied. "Didn't you tell me you were all those things?"

"I did, but I didn't tell you everything."

"Oh, that'll do."

During those hours of flying, and those hours of dreadful silence, when there was nothing to say, Cristina had the time to become self-conscious. At last, she had the time to wonder how she should be. What attitude? What kind of woman would he like?

"I'm old, you know," she said, just so he wouldn't ask her how old she was.

"Relative to what?"

"To time itself. I'm thirty-four," she lied.

In truth she was thirty-six, but she thought she could pass for thirty-four, easily.

"Thirty-four!" he said. "Relax! You're fine."

"You really think so?" she asked. But it didn't seem as if he wanted to talk about it.

After they had claimed their luggage and gone through customs, Frederick-Charles said, "See you around!" Cristina thought it was because of her age. Oh, she shouldn't have told him! Why only shave two years off when you're lying?!

"Frederick-Charles! Frederick-Charles!" she yelled before he hopped on a cab. "I lied about my age. I'm thirty-two. Do you think I'm old?"

"Hell, no! You're fine! See you around!"

Two weeks later, they were in Nicaragua. And Cristina was still wondering how she should act. He sure didn't seem to need a Mommy, much less someone to tell him what to do, or to help him, or to cook dinner for him. The only thing he seemed to care about were his bells, and he probably didn't need someone to polish them. He didn't seem to need a place to sleep either. He had his own loft, twice the size of hers from what she'd heard. So, if he ever saw hers he wouldn't even be impressed. Moreover, he never asked any questions, so she was completely in the dark as to where she stood, what she had to do.

In Panama she panicked. What should she be? What should she do? She sulked. He didn't notice. She yelled at one of the people from her crew. He didn't notice either. Then she tried to look sad. Maybe she'd seem mysterious. He didn't notice that either. There she was, thirty-six years old and dying to marry, and the man she was madly in love with was slipping like a bar of soap between her hands. She cried and felt nauseous with impatience. One minute she swore that it absolutely had to work this time. The next minute she was planting a banner of defeat on her forehead. She was unlucky. "I'm unlucky. I'm unlucky. No luck," she said to herself. She thought she wanted what she could never have and was over-whelmed by this, her personal tragedy.

To make matters worse, after she returned to New York, two weeks passed and no news from Frederick-Charles. At the station she'd jump on her phone every time it would buzz, but it was never him. The same at home. She took to running to the phone every ten minutes or so. Perhaps the cat had unhooked it. She even gave instructions to Paloma, the live-in maid she had brought home with her the evening she told her father she never wanted to see him again. The fight had begun over Paloma, who was then employed at her parents'. Upon hearing that Paloma had inadvertently broken several of his Tiffany's porcelain tulips, Cristina's father had run into the maid's room, yelled at poor Paloma, grabbed her prayer book, ripped it to pieces, and trampled on it. Cristina had wit-nessed this scene. When she walked into the maid's room to see what was going on, her father was jumping up and down on the torn pages of the prayer book. So it was her turn to yell, to call her father all sorts of nasty names, and to storm out of the house, taking Paloma with her.

The problem was that Paloma didn't speak a word of English and that the minute the answering machine went on, the cat ran and put her paw on the "off" button. Cristina even thought about getting rid of that selfish cat. But since the cat was another one of her father's victims, she had no choice but to keep her. It was a matter of principle.

So, Cristina ended up repeating the name Frederick-Charles to Paloma every time she got a chance and giving her instructions that if she even remotely heard any vowels and consonants that remotely sounded like Frederick-Charles on the phone, she was to call her, wherever she was.

"Si, Señora," Paloma said. Whether she understood or not, and whether she'd comply or not, "Si, Señora," was the only thing Paloma ever said.

A month passed, still no news from Frederick-Charles. So Cristina, the conquering Cristina, decided to pay him a visit. His loft was on Varick Street. As she approached the building, her imagination—imagination being the worst of evils and the worst of enemies—tried exhausting all the possibilities of what the outcome of this surprise visit would be. If he was alone in his loft, he'd probably be glad to see her. If he was working or playing his bells, she'd probably disturb him. If he had a woman with him, he'd be embarrassed. If he was away, nobody would answer the doorbell—unless he lived with someone. What if he was there and didn't answer the doorbell? Anyway, he would either be busy, or alone, or with a woman, or away. These were the possibilities. Nothing else could happen. Cristina wanted to be in full control and ready for everything. She wasn't going to be let down. She wasn't. She was intent on that.

At least she thought she had exhausted all the possibilities. When the elevator door opened to another closed door, she read a sign that said, "Please ring this bell hard." She could almost hear his voice while she read it. Underneath was another bell, and another sign. It read, "Please don't ring this bell hard." And there was a third sign: "If the elevator door begins to close, please put your foot in it." Cristina rang both doorbells and put her foot in front of the elevator door, just in case. She wanted to be in full control of the situation.

"Oh, it's you. Come in. I'm quite glad to see you," Frederick-Charles' soft British voice said. "Please come in. Please do come in."

So if he was glad to see her, he wasn't with a woman, and he wasn't busy, maybe she'd won. For a minute she thought she was Cortés standing in front of all the Aztec gold. "Would you like some hot apple cider?" he asked. "You came just at the right time. Neza's making hot apple cider right now."

She didn't quite understand the name he had uttered. It was dim in his loft. But she did discern a woman in the kitchen; the second elevator door opened to the kitchen. "Am I disturbing you?" she asked. "No, not at all," he replied. "Here, meet Nezahual. Nezahual meet Cristina."

She certainly had an exotic name. Cristina wondered if she was younger or older than she. It was dim in his loft, but she thought she saw strands of white hair on this woman's head. Was she old? She must come from an exotic place. With a name like that she could come from Mars. It was just like Frederick-Charles to fall in love with an exotic woman. Next thing you know, he'll be saying, "she's my wife." But he never said that.

"Hi!" what's her name said. "Frederick-Charles had told me a lot about you." So Frederick-Charles was going to turn out just like Aaron. Next thing you know she'll be saying, "You're just like a mother to him." But she didn't say that.

Wasn't anything that she expected to see or hear or experience going to happen? Cristina didn't want surprises.

Horror of horrors. Bad luck. Plain bad luck. What's her name had bleached several strands of her hair white. That meant she had to be very young. Women in their thirties don't do that. "What's that I hear?" Cristina asked without taking her eyes off whatever it was her name was. "Oh, those are my bells!' Frederick-Charles said. "I put them on automatic. Come! Do come watch!"

Cristina followed him, and when she saw it, she exclaimed, "Oh, it looks just like the sculpture at Port Authority. Except that it has bells instead of billiard balls. Curious. Curious contraption. And big." She walked around it.

Nezahual joined them. She was carrying a tray with three mugs full of hot apple cider. Cristina took one and immediately turned to Frederick-Charles and said, "Actually, this reminds me of those gigantic Calder mobiles." You never know, perhaps this woman here had a ten-point lead on youth, but not on culture.

"And are these all Tibetan bells?" Cristina asked.

"Oh, not at all," he said. "This one here's a souvenir from Switzerland. A cow bell. Those there are chimes. You can call these jingle bells...but most of them are Tibetan bells."

"Why aren't they ringing anymore?"

"Oh, but they are. Sometimes the range is so wide that you can't hear the sound."

"And how long have you known Frederick-Charles?" Cristina turned to what's her name and asked.

"I don't remember."

"Oh. And you're not from here, I suppose."

"No. I'm from Jersey."

"Oh," Cristina said. "With a name like that I thought you'd be Indian or even...Tibetan! Like these bells here! Ha-ha?"

"Well, Nezahual's my professional name. In reality I'm an historian, but since I can't make a living with that, *tú sabes*, I give these massages that take pain away, and Nezahual's the name I use for giving the massages. It's a long story."

"Well, you're young," Cristina hinted. "You'll have time to make money as an historian. You're very young, aren't you?"

"Not really. I'm twenty-four."

Cristina suddenly wanted to sit down. Frederick-Charles told her she was welcome to the floor. All three sat down next to the eight-foot sculpture.

"Your back hurts, doesn't it?" Neza asked Cristina in Spanish.

"My back?! Yes! But I'm used to it," Cristina replied. "It's nothing. It's not my age or anything. I've had this pain forever."

"Here, lie down on your stomach. I'll give you a massage," Neza suggested. "They're special massages."

"Oh, I'm fine really, I swear. Besides, it's a family thing. We don't believe in relaxation and massages. If you ask my father, he'll tell you all this is rubbish. You're not supposed to relax. It makes you waste time. And I certainly hate to waste time. Oh! I like that bell! I haven't talked to my father in years though. I should though, because another one of my brothers is dying. The people in my family are dying like flies! It's not funny; I didn't mean it as a joke. It really bothers me. We're dying while the Bos family — on my mother's side — is multiplying. Oh, O.K., if you insist. You say I should lie on my stomach? If you insist. But it won't do me any good. My back always hurts. It's because of the way I live, I mean sit. Now, how is it done? How should I lie down?"

"There's only one way to lie down," Neza said. "And that's comfortably."

"Comfortably?" Cristina asked, as if she'd never heard that word in her life. "Really, I don't need to be comfortable. You're the one who should be comfortable. You're doing the work, giving the massage. Oh, my God, that bell! You say I'm tense? That bell just reminded me of something terrible! And that one! They're my years passing! I really should get out of here. They're at twenty-nine! Thirty! Thirty-one! I'm sorry I'm talking so much. Perhaps I should keep quiet?"

Then the bells started ringing her men. Fujiwara, Mark...Carlos and his mother! Take that bell away! Aaron. Angel. And that one sounded like her. And this one was her impatient love for Frederick-Charles. And what was that one? So sweet. What time was it? Four-o'clock in the morning? Already? Had she fallen asleep? Was she sick? Why this sweetness? And where was her impatience? Her mad rush. Her fear of the passing years. Her fear of failure. Her envy. No man? Still not yet? Oh, that bell. But where was her love? Where were her mad passions? How could she survive without them? Was it yet another sign that she was getting older? Where was her love for Frederick-Charles? And how did it ring? Oh, she was no longer in love, no envy now, she had let go.

The Battery-Operated Drummer Bear

I

Frank Carbone became a millionaire back in the 1950s thanks to this brilliant idea he had of advertising Golden Lady Soft Drinks and Juices to the Spanish-speaking people who were already in New York and New Jersey at that time. Shortly thereafter, by dint of seventeen-hour days, cunning, and ever-growing megalomania, he also got the King and Queen Food account which included milk, several shapes of pasta, and a colorful line of gelatins and puddings. It wasn't long before Golden Lady Inc. was sponsoring community baseball games and King and Queen Food Inc. was distributing free pudding samples in street fairs commemorating Spanish heritage events. By then, Carbone had already invented the term "Spanish market."

Thirty-eight years after his triumph, Carbone still bragged about how he had come up with this idea all by himself—advertising and marketing to Hispanics—and fondly remembered those good old days when he had a half-hour long tv show right after *I Love Lucy*, a half-hour to make the Spanish-speaking people laugh while telling them what food products to buy. And though his one-man show was on national tv for only two years or so, Carbone's ego and pride soon multiplied these two years by five, then by six, then by seven, and finally by a whole lifetime. But there was some truth in that. Carbone was indeed a one-man show. He'd always been so.

Carbone also bragged about being from what he called the old school of business, that is, all work and no leisure—vacations being for the dying and the ill—and foul words and yelling and stomping, and just enough of a family life to produce an alcoholic wife and four children whose lives had gone sour. There was, however, a fifth child, a girl, Cristina, Carbone's pride and joy, whom he hadn't seen for three years. The day after his seventieth birthday, she told him she never wanted to have anything to do with him again. Carbone's lisping dated back to that sad day, or at least that's what Gumersindo Osorio, Don Gume for short—a Puerto Rican who had been with Carbone since the very beginning—said.

Carbone's office is in a gray, shabby building on the corner of Summit and Sip Avenues, within walking distance from the Journal Square Station, in the bustling, restless, industrious, as well as homeless and unemployed, heart of a Jersey City neighborhood mainly composed of Hispanics, Indians, Arabs, Pakistani, and Blacks. Don Gume is forever making fun of the building that contains the offices of Carbone & Associates. After saying and repeating that the building's as old as Carbone and as disheveled as his head, he laughs and coughs all by himself. And it's no better inside, he adds, once he's stopped coughing and laughing. The elevators, for example, hardly ever work. Four days a week, the six steady employees of Carbone & Associates have to take the stairs. But this isn't too bad, for the office is on the second floor, just one flight up. This means that the six steady employees of Carbone & Associates work to the din of this undecided New Jersey town. It's noisy even when the gray, dusty, guillotine windows are shut. Actually, most of them have either been nailed or painted shut, and it's only in the interstices of these windows that the adolescent paint in this office seems to hold.

The only two windows that slide up and down are in Frank Carbone's office. This is normal since Frank Carbone is the King, the Despot, the Boss, the Ruler. He should have the best therefore. The others don't need air. Why should they? And why should they complain? Isn't he paying them?

It goes without saying that Frank Carbone's advertising business began and will most probably see its end in this building. This is where he had made millions, and at the age of seventy-three still planned to make millions more. So he clung on to this building as if it were a lucky pen, and as its sole owner, he refused to make any turn-of-the-century improvements. Inside the building it smells of stale pencil, old paper, and dusty file cabinets, the kind you only see in thrift shops. His only concession to modernity is the red, white and blue express-mail box. Were it not for this box, you'd be walking right into the fifties, right into one of those places where intolerant old men, who believed in all work and no play, made enough money to keep the two ensuing generations going. In other words, Frank Carbone, that loud, foul-mouthed creature who claims to have invented Hispanic advertising, as well as Hispanics, could double as anyone's despotic daddy or granddaddy.

He always argued that nothing was wrong with his building, that the objective was to make money and not to spend ten hours a day twiddling your thumbs in a plush office. Furthermore, if something didn't need fixing, why the hell spend the money? This is why the plastic yellowed letters that fell from the building directory in the lobby were never replaced. The CAR had fallen off of CARBONE, the OC. off of ASSOC., the result being that it now read "BONE & ASS first floor." Carbone had seen it and it made him laugh every time he passed by. He said that the important thing was that the "Number One in Spanish Advertising, Marketing, and Public Relations" right below it remain intact.

Another one of his eccentricities was the battery-operated drummer bear on his desk. His daughter Cristina, just a day before having taken her daughterly love away from him, had put it on the blue meringue cake she had brought to the office for Carbone's seventieth birthday party. Once in a while, he activated it. It made him laugh. He resembled a child who's inspecting a toy for the first time. Those were the only times he seemed like a sweet little old man. Sometimes, when Carbone would pound with anger on his desk, the bear would go off by itself. He'd stop for a minute and smile, then go back to his ranting and raving. He'd strictly forbidden anyone to touch that bear and had hollered that whosoever disobeyed his order he'd terminate on the spot and use physical force if he had to.

It was another one of those long, hot summers. Everyone was sweltering in the office and the air was so thick that even the twenty-year-old fans refused to go at high speed. Carbone had stopped coming in at six a.m. because one of his sons was dying at Christ Hospital. He started coming in at two, which accounted for the "when-the-cat's-not-home-the-mice-dance" atmosphere in the office until fifteen minutes before his esti-mated arrival. The mice danced cautiously though, for Don Gume, the Black Puerto Rican who had been with Carbone

almost from the very beginning, had the reputation of being a
tattle-tale. Perhaps he was, perhaps he wasn't; the important
thing was that this mouse here, this Don Gume mouse, with
the reputation he had, could do whatever he wanted. And he,
therefore, spent a whole canicular Monday morning gossiping
with the new account executive that Carbone had just hired.

"You'll see...." Don Gume wiped the sweat off his brow and
continued hassling the new account executive who was fresh
from a two-name and strictly-Anglo advertising agency. While
he was gossiping, he was also pointing toward the ceiling with
his index finger that resembled a worn-out leather glove. "I
know," he raised his voice, raised his brow, and carried on. "I
have counted four-hundred and sixty-three employees since I
start to work for Carbone thirty-eight years ago," and he
popped the cap off the jumbo red magic marker when he pro-
nounced the word "ago."

He then slipped his half-moon glasses on and appraised
the faint pencil markings on the glossy white two-by-three
illustration board. "Yes," he scratched his chin. "Thirty-eight
year already. The day I come here from Puerto Rico I estart to
work for Carbone. So I know Frank very well," he muttered,
with his eyes still glued to the illustration board. "Is hot here,
no? Wait, in August it get even worse. Anyway, Frank even go
to look for his executives in Alcoholics Anonymous. He know
that a normal person no accept pay under the table with no
medical benefit," he said, and put his hand under the table,
pretending to be handing the new account executive her pay.
"And you he hire because you American and come from American advertising agency and you desperate. I hear the big
American agency fire you, yes or no?"

"They laid me off," the new girl named Laurie corrected
him. "When we lost the..." she started to say.

""Yeah, yeah," Don Gume interrupted Laurie. "Is not
important, but please know that he take you to see King
Backer in a month maybe, if you last, to show Backer that he
no only hire alcoholics and crazy pee-pol but normal Americans, too," he said and wiped the sweat off his brow again.
"And I don't think you make good impression on Backer.
Backer no like skinny girls," he waved bye-bye at her. "Backer
no is brand manager," he waved his index finger. "Frank
refuse to deal with brand manager because he say president
only deal with president. And King Backer is big president of

King and Queen Food." He raised both his arms then lowered them to the sides. "Frank always take him to Italian restaurant on upper east side and talk about his children who are no good and cost him a lot of money. All of them except Cristina, who just have bad character and is too snob to come here to Jersey City. You think King Backer accept advertising budget because Carbone do good work? Never!" he brushed an invisible fly away. "King Backer get forty-thousand dollar a year from Carbone. And I tell you because is no big secret."

"I really don't want to hear this," the new account executive said.

"You want I put the fan in you direction?"

"No, thank you, but I'd love it if you put your smelly cigarette out."

Dom Gume paid no attention. He let the cigarette continue smoking in the Bacardi Rum ashtray all by itself. His fingers were fondling the cap of the jumbo marker. With the other hand, he straightened the illustration board and rechecked the pencil markings. Then he groped for the jumbo marker that had already slipped beneath the mess on his desk.

The smelly tip touched the glossy surface; it creaked at the curve of the letters. The finished product read:

> King and Queen Food Salutes the
> Hispanic Community of Jersey City, New Jersey
> Come try delicious samples! Free!
> Absolutely FREE! No obligation!!

Don Gume's corner was reminiscent of cafeterias whose four walls are lined with picture postcards, autographed photos of long-forgotten stars, wilted foreign currency bills, buntings, and oriflammes. Right behind him, he had thumbtacked photos of past Puerto Rican Day parades to the wood paneling. Some were half-torn, others were curling up, all were faded versions of pompous floats and Hispanic queens of the day, in fluffy dresses, waving their scepters at the bystanders. On the other side of the wall, there was a plastic Puerto Rican coat of arms and Frank Carbone's photo wrapped in Handy Wrap. It was a photo from twenty-five years ago, when Carbone, in his heyday, was still old. Right beneath it, somebody had written in red "And I created Hispanics on the eighth day."

"Carbone going down," Don Gume breathed out. "He is going to lose the Golden Girl account because he fool around," he added, and then reached toward a grimy alarm-clock radio and turned the sound up. The room was unexpectedly filled with a Spanish live broadcast of a baseball game, interrupted, now and then, by an announcer reminding us that we were listening to Radio Piñata on the AM dial.

"Why you look at me that way?" Don Gume asked the new Anglo account executive. "You want to work? I bother you? You serious person? We no like serious pee-pol here. And you have to adapt to new culture, no? Is a plus for you future. And is you first day here, and is very hot. Take it easy. I tell you, Carbone steal too much."

"I really don't want to hear this, Mr. Gumeee," the new girl said. "I'm busy; I have a lot of work to do. Oh, my God, it's so hot! Can't we open a window?"

"They no open, and I tell you," Don Gume carried on. "Carbone think he can do whatever he want with Golden Girl. Take example, when he make promotion for Golden Girl in Colombia Heritage Festival, he charge client eight-thousand dollar, and what he pay? I tell you. One-hundred-thirty dollar for me to do promotion," he said and stuck his pinky finger out. "Twenty-five dollar for hostess with the hat and the sash," he said, this time sticking his ring finger out and then putting one hand on his head and the other on his chest. "The radio station," he said with the pinky, ring, and middle finger of his right hand stretched out while pointing to the alarm-clock radio with his left hand, "give him kiosk for free with the merchandising. So he pay a total of one-hundred and sixty-five dollar. I make photographer come to take photos, and Carbone refuse to pay. I make musician come, and Carbone refuse to pay. I ask for batteries for radio," again, he pointed to the alarm-clock radio, "and Carbone refuse to buy. You, who come from big American agency, you call that promotion? I no call that promotion. Carbone is like virus who kill the body that feed it. He want to milk cow until cow dead, then he cry because cow is dead. Golden Girl is a dead cow," Don Gume said, and pointed to Carbone's photo wrapped in Handy Wrap. "Today, instead of going to the hospital because his son is dying, Carbone have meeting in New York City for Golden Girl Account. You will see when he come back. He is going to lose the account. He is going to lose the account because the secret is not only in kick-back." He went through all the mimics of a whisper. "You have to give service to the client and not allow you brother-in-law to put the White-Out on the bills and change numbers. You no believe? What you think Don Gonzalo do all day back there? Exactly, he put White-Out on the bills. That is his job. Big job!"

"Mr. Gumeee, this does not interest me," the American girl said to him. "Mr. Gumeee, I am not used to hearing this kind of thing, nor do I want to hear it."

Just then, Carbone walked into the office accompanied by a tall, skinny man. "Look! Is Clare Kelly! He have a lot of problems with alcohol!" Don Gume whispered nervously as if this Clare Kelly were some kind of movie star. Behind them, a short, blond-haired young man entered. "Is Dave! He need panty; he no need boxer shorts!" Don Gume went through all the same mimics again.

"Hello, Don Gume," Carbone said. "Hello, Mememe...Lelele," he hesitated.

"Laurie Abrams," she said.

"Oh, yes, hello, Laurie Abrams," he remembered. "Ho-ho! Laurie Abrams, ho-ho!"

"How it go, Frank?" Don Gume asked.

"It doesn't look good, Don Gume, it doesn't look good," he uttered before turning around and walking away.

"Where did we go wrong, Ccclare?" Carbone asked Clare when they were halfway down the corridor.

"What do you think happened?" Laurie asked Don Gume.

"Sshh!" Don Gume answered. "Here is plywood," he said, and knocked on the wood paneling. "Here you no ask. You listen."

"Hello, Mr. Carbone. How did the meeting with Golden Girl go?" the girl named Silviana asked her boss.

You could hear them clearly even though they were in the rear offices now.

"Nnnnot very good, honey, nnnot very good," Carbone replied. "I told them to take one of thththeir Golden Girl bottles and shove it up thththeir rear extremity."

"Oh, I'm so sorry to hear that, Mr. Carbone!" the girl named Silviana whined.

"Whwhwhere did we ggo wrong, Cclare?" Carbone asked this man named Clare.

"Frank, we really need an air conditioner in here..." the man named Clare started to say.

"Fffu...ing aaaa," Carbone continued. "Excuse the language, Sssilviana, honey. "Tell me, Clare, what the hell do they know about the fffu...ing Spanish mamamarket? TV! They want TV! Don't they realize Hispanics don't watch TV?! Your typical lalalatino doesn't watch TV! Golden Girl has nothing but a bunch of yuppie queers working for them! When I started with Golden Girl thirty-five years ago, Hispanics preferred to drink New Jersey swamp water rararather than Golden Girl. They were down here! I got them up there! I made them number one! Get me a cup of coffee, Silviana, honey. Because we are number one! We're number one in Spanish advertising! The secret is in community events. How many times have have haven't I expatiated on that subject, Clare?!"

"This place's as hot as a laundromat, Frank. When are we going to get an..." the man named Clare started to ask.

"Don't interrupt me, Ccclare. Latinos like to be outside, and every time they see a crowd they join in. Ugh, so the only way to reach them is through community events. Thank you, Silviana, honey. Oh, honey, the next time I tell you to send my dentures over with the security guard, send me both plates. I only got the upper one today. Let me take this damn thing off. It hurts like hell. Come into my office, Clare. No, we're not getting an air conditioner. It'll just make the electric bill sky high and . . ."

"Now you cannot hear no more, they shut the door," Don Gume whispered to Laurie Abrams.

"I never eavesdrop," Laurie Abrams said. "Boy, it sure is hot in here!"

"What I tell you? This is the system here. Frank refuse to pay twenty-five extra dollar to have musician with guitar in promotion. Laura, how you want I make good mini-event like that?"

"My name's Laurie," she corrected him. "Mr. Gumee, I'd really like to get some work done."

"Take example," Don Gume carried on. "One time, my wife, Virginia—you meet her soon—one time she make pudding for the mini-event. I put it in station wagon and everything spill in my car. This make Frank laugh. Then he send tree-hundred dollar a day for each of his boys, who are big men now. Not for the girl. Frank prefer the boys. Diana Lynn is obliged to come here every month and beg for money. He is very hard with Diana Lynn. She is no good, too, but Frank no want to believe it. And Cristina no like Jersey City. She no like her family and she no like her pee-pol. She is a famous journalist with much talent and she is pretty, pretty, pretty and too snob to come here."

"Don Gumee, you're really driving me crazy! And this heat! These are lousy working conditions. Please stop!"

Don Gume laughed and turned the radio up.

"Well! Something has to be done about this and right away!" Laurie Abrams prissily stood up and said.

"And ask Frank for air conditioner, too!" he said sardonically.

She walked out of the office that she shared with Don Gume and shot one last glance at him, like a school teacher who's about to get the principal. She walked past the water cooler, down the plastic carpet that protects the old brick colored rug. The walls of the corridor are lined with Frank Carbone's plaques in recognition for services rendered to the Hispanic Community, to the Union City domino club, to the handicapped children of West New York, to the Jersey City bingo club.

Don Gonzalo's office was just as stuffed and stuffy as everyone else's. Gorged bookcases, metal file cabinets, one brown wilted thing equilibrating on another and counterbalancing yet another. He was propped behind a stronghold of greenish heavyweight ledgers. They let out a pungent smell of skin disease and stale pencils. Sprawling about, an army of little plastic bottles. White, green, pink, blue liquid paper. Some little bottles were standing, others were down, and in several, the liquid had become so thick that you could only shove the little brush halfway in. When Laurie Abrams sat down in front of Don Gonzalo, he was niggardly trying to smooth out the disheveled little bristles of one of the brushes.

"This is shit!" he murmured.

"Mr. Gonzalo," Laurie Abrams said. "I don't want to disturb Mr. Carbone because he's in a meeting with Mr. Kelly, but he told me on Friday that I should come and see you if there were any problems. Could you please tell Mr. Gumee to keep quiet and turn the radio off so I can get my work done?"

The little brush looked like an unkempt head of hair. Don Gonzalo squeezed the bristles with his thumb and forefinger, but every time he let go, the thing was just as before. Don Gonzalo had age stains on his hands and yellow nails.

"The problem here is that nobody cares," the old man said. "The people you see out there, wasting their time, listening to Radio Piñata, those same ones, they take a yellow piece of paper like this, write one little thing on it that takes up half-a-line, then they crumple it up," he yelled and crumpled the yellow piece of paper up, "and throw it away!" he said, and just to make his point, picked up the waste-paper basket and threw the yellow ball of paper in there. "Do you know how many unused lines are left?" he asked. Some spit fell on the green ledger. "Twenty-seven and a half in the front and twenty-eight in the back!" he answered his own question. "You can't run a business this way!" he pounded on the ledger, two bottles of White-Out fell. "There's too much waste! Frank Carbone comes in at two o'clock. He doesn't know...He has too many personal problems. This poor man..." Don Gonzalo paused and seemed to have lost his train of thought.

"Do you think I can go in and talk to Mr. Carbone?" Laurie asked Don Gonzalo as if she had just mistaken a patient for a doctor in an insane asylum.

"Today is not a good day. I heard the bear," Don Gonzalo said.

"You what?" asked Laurie with a weary voice.

"The bear on his desk. A little thing this high that runs with batteries and plays the drums. It goes off by itself whenever Carbone pounds on his desk, and that means he's in a very bad mood. And right before you came in here, I heard it. If ever you take anything from my desk," he said, out of the blue. "I will ask you, please, to put it back, immediately."

Then he went back to the disheveled little brush and tried to comb the bristles with his one long finger nail. Laurie cleared her throat and waited, but this man was obviously too busy. Without another word, she stood up and left.

II

On Tuesday Carbone called a meeting just when everybody was getting ready to go home. Laurie Abrams, being new and still serious about her new job, was the first one in the conference room. She had two sharpened pencils, a brand new eraser, and a yellow pad, as if she were going to take one of those multiple-choice exams. Then Clare walked in with a brown More cigarette dangling from his mouth. Behind him was Don Gume, dressed to a tee, smelling of after-shave and talcum powder. Two minutes later a young man named Gustavo appeared. Laurie sat at the end of the table next to Clare who was shaking a brand new More out of the long, red, skinny pack. Silviana came in, sat down, and scribbled the date on the upper right hand corner of a loose-leaf, college-ruled piece of paper. Gustavo started complaining that it was already five twenty-five. Don Gonzalo walked in and sat on a plastic chair, not one of the matching ones. He eyed moping Gustavo who was sadistically stabbing the arm of one of the conference room armchairs with a bitten Bic pen. Don Gonzalo shook his head in disapproval. Carbone wasn't in the conference room yet. He was still in his office, ranting and raving on the phone, calling someone a no good drug addict.

DON'T YOU DARE COME TO THIS OFFICE, YOU ADDICT!!! Carbone roared then slammed the receiver down.

A minute later he was in the conference room, refreshed and smelling of after-shave. The different smells of men's perfumes filled the place.

"This is no way to run a business," Don Gonzalo complained to Silviana.

"Gonzalo," Carbone uttered, like an irritated schoolmaster.

"You can't mix your personal life with your professional..." Don Gonzalo carried on.

"Gggonzalo," Carbone repeated. "Everyone! Listen to me! Cclare! Dddave! Sssilviana, honey, turn that fan down, will you?! No wonder the electric bill's sky-high at this time of year! It it it doesn't need to be on high! Gggustavo! Pepeput your hands on the table! Whawhawhat are you doing? Dddon't lean your your chair against the the the wall. You're scratching the wood paneling. This place is a conference room, and I want nobody here unless they expressly have my permission to come in here. And that goes for you, Clare...You you you all have desks. Gggonzalo, will you put a sign up on this door forbidding anyone to come in here? If I catch any one of you in here without my permission, I will terminate you on the spot and use physical force if I have to..."

"Frank," Clare interrupted.

"Clare, you have this ill habit of interrupting me when I'm not finished!"

"Frank, it's quarter to six! Let's get on with the meeting!"

"Ugh!" Carbone swallowed. "Oh, O.K., staff. I ggot a call last Friday from a chap named Stanley Robinson, executive VP of Purple Advertising and, ugh, these guys want our help! Ho! Ho! They know we're the best! Ho! Ho! You've probably all heard of Purple Advertising. They have a billing of one and a half billion—correct me if I'm wrong, Clare. And don't forget they're the ones who called us, we didn't call them. They know! Nice chap, this Stanleyleyley Levine. Young chap. Lives right here in Jersey. Knows the area well, and he he he wawawawants to come over and take a look at our offices. Purple Advertising is probably aware by now that they can't, ugh, eschew the Hispanic market. Do you know what that means, Silviana, honey, the word eschew? It's a ninety-four billion dollar market, not counting the illegals. So you can multiply that ninety-four billion dollar figure by two. One out of two Latinos are illegals! It's in their blood! Like pride is in their blood!" Carbone hollered. "So Stanleyleyley Harrison from Purple Advertising has most likely perused these census bureau facts, and ugh, ugh, we probably caught their eye in the Red Book, and, ugh, they need us! Ho! Ho!" Carbone guffawed. "They probably want us to take them by the hand and lead them, ugh...Show them the way into this three-hundred billion dollar market, not counting the illegals, so you can multiply that three-hundred-dollar figure by two. Ugh, Purple Advertising knows about us. They know we're number one! MarmarmeIsCrisLeleLolo..."

"Laurie Abrams," she said.

"I'd like to welcome Lololaurie Abrams on board! Lololaurie, honey, you'll soon find out that we're not like other Hispanic advertising agencies that translate Anglo commercials into Spanish. We think in Spanish! I I I know the Latino mind. I forged the Latino mind! You you you can't get through to them with an Anglo message! And you can't get through to them with an Anglo medium either! So the only way to get through to them is through community events!" Carbone guffawed again. "Don Gume, we have to get, what's it called, Ple-

pledge? For the wood paneling. Get those scratches out, will you, Don Gume? The man from Purple's coming on Friday at five-thirty. And will you get some rug shampoo, too? That day, staff, I want your desks cleared..."

"Frank!" Clare interrupted.

"Wait until I'm finished, Clare. Nnnot completely cleared, you you you have to make them think someone's sitting there. And nnnot that you don't already look good, but I wawawant you to dress up, and that goes for you, Gustavo. Wear a suit, O.K.? Lololaurie, honey, you're fine with what you're wearing right now. Silviana, honey, get some plants. Dave, you're the art director. Can we make any room here look like an art department? Get all the old work out of the stock room. And you, Gustavo, go through our old video tapes and choose the best commercials...Ho! Ho! There sure are some good ones in there! The ones we did for King and Queen Food in my back yard, remember, Don Gume? Ho! Ho! I'm getting some new people on board. There's a new typist coming in tomorrow. That'll relieve you, Silviana, honey. We're also getting a new account executive, a Cuban chap. Let's all work together, O.K., staff? If Purple Advertising gives us their business, that'll mean Christmas bonuses for all you you. This chap's coming on Friday, exactly three days from today. Let's all be prepared, O.K.?"

III

Don Gume bought the Pledge. Silviana bought African Queens, Ponytail palms, and rubber plants. They looked nice. Dave and Clare made sure they had a good stock of business cards. Don Gume wiped the sweat from his brow while dusting the Puerto Rican coat of arms. Gustavo hollered that Purple was the chance of a lifetime. He also said that Purple Advertising was going to make all these wasted years at Carbone & Associates worthwhile. He kept wondering if Purple was coming here to buy Carbone out...or to search for new talent?

By Wednesday morning everyone except Don Gume and Laurie Abrams had fresh up-to-date copies of their resumés ready to be slipped into the hand of the man from Purple the minute Carbone turned his back. Schemes such as these made Don Gume laugh. He asked several of his co-workers how they'd react if they went into the drugstore across the street to browse and suddenly all the employees fell to their knees with outstretched arms and handed them their resumés, portfolios, and calling cards.

"This is like a *bodega*," Don Gume teeheed. "And full of crazy pee-pol! But at least a *bodega* have air conditioner!"

"It's people like you who turn it into a bowdaygo," Laurie Abrams turned to Don Gume and said. "And please stop blowing that cigarette smoke in my face. I'm allergic!"

Just then, Don Prudencio, the security guard, walked in and told Laurie that Carbone wanted to see her right away. Don Gume puffed some more smoke out and coughed and laughed at the same time.

Past the water cooler, down the plastic carpet . . . "Sit down, honey," Carbone said to Laurie when she walked into his office. The ashes from Clare's More fell on the rug, and Silviana was desperately searching for something in a file drawer. "Whawhawhat are you working on, honey?" Carbone asked Laurie.

"A media analysis for Beneficial Betting," Laurie answered.

"Wha wha wha," he puffed. "What the hell for?"

"It's in the proposal," she replied. "I consulted this with Mr. Kelly, and he agreed that this media analysis should be number one on my list."

"Wha wha wha," Carbone puffed some more. "Who the hell's Clare to agree with you?! Clare! Wha wha why'd you agree that she waste her time on this?"

"Frank . . . "

"Don't interrupt me, Clare. Where do you think we are, honey, on Madison Avenue? I give Beneficial Betting enough money as it is, and I'm not paying you to waste your time on this. Besides, we've got a media analysis in each and every file cabinet. Didn't we do one for King and Queen Food, Clare?"

"In 1965, Frank," Clare said casually. "Those numbers are a little stale now. Frank. We really gotta get this media analysis to Beneficial Betting. It's in the proposal."

"Oh. O.K.," Carbone reluctantly said. "But next time, honey," he told Laurie, "You ask me. I'm the boss. Now run along."

"Mr. Carbone, I thought I'd take this opportunity to discuss some problems with you," Laurie said.

"Not now, honey, I'm busy, run along. Run along!"

Half-an-hour later when Laurie was walking toward the Journal Square Path Station, a man named Nick ran up to her brandishing a white envelope. "Hi, sweetheart, I'm Nick," he said. "You don't know me, but I work for Carbone, too."

He brandished the white envelope in front of her face again and begged her to take it to Carbone's son who, according to what he'd heard, lived only two blocks away from her. The address was scribbled on the Carbone & Associates envelope. All Laurie had to do was give it to the doorman with a wrinkled dollar that this man named Nick took out of his shirt pocket. He begged and begged and explained that he was expected somewhere and that Carbone's son needed this envelope this evening. Could Laurie do that favor for him? Of course, there was no need to tell Carbone about this. All she had to do was give the envelope to the doorman. That was it! Laurie said that she wasn't going straight home, that she had an aerobics class, and was meeting some friends after that, but she could give this envelope to the doorman at around half-past nine, was that all right? "That's perfect, sweetheart," Nick replied. "You're an angel. You're a sweetheart! By the way, has anyone told you that you look just like Cristina? Cristina Carbone. O.K., O.K., I won't keep you. You'll be late for your aerobics class. Thanks and see you soon!"

IV

On Thursday afternoon Carbone came in an hour earlier than usual. He caught Gustavo with his feet on his desk, a half-finished crossword puzzle on his lap, and the loud words "tomorrow's the big day!" in his mouth. He caught Silviana up in the front desk making a personal phone call. He caught Clare going through the employment section of Ad-Week. He caught Don Gume listening to Radio Piñata with the sound all the way up, Don Prudencio, the security guard, playing darts with sharpened pencils, and Dave tending to his own personal business matters. The only two serious people were Don Gonzalo, who was daubing bills with White-Out, and

Laurie Abrams, who seemed forever working on that media analysis.

"Laurie!" Carbone said. "Come into my office right away!"

Don Gume, who was fanning himself with a notepad, turned the radio down and waved bye-bye at her. She followed the boss past the water cooler, down the plastic carpet, and into his office. "Sit down," he said, and threw his attaché case on his desk so hard that the drummer bear banged on the drums three times. Suddenly Carbone's expression changed. He turned to the bear and smiled, like a child discovering a toy for the first time. "Isn't it cute? Look at its paws! Cutest thing I've ever seen! Ho! Ho!"

Then his expression changed again. Out of the wrinkled, gelatinous skin around his lips (for he had no teeth) came a roaring YESTERDAY. Laurie jumped. Then still another YESTERDAY! He fumbled for his words and finally proceeded with his sentence.

"I gave an order to one of my employees, an order which was not duly executed," he whispered. "And why was this order transgressed?!" he bawled. "Because you plotted," he mumbled, "schemed," (a little louder) "and connived," he barked, some spit fell on Laurie's hand, "with my employee. Against me! Your boss! And do you know what the aftermath of this contumacy was?" he muttered. "My son and his wife didn't get their money on time! Don't 'but' me, Laurie Abrams. I warn you, I will not condone your vile act!" he shrieked, he sputtered, and whammed the suction-grip pencil sharpener. The drummer bear went off again. Carbone turned his head toward it and smiled.

"He just asked me to do him a favor," Laurie protested.

The smile on Carbone's face suddenly metamorphosed into a loud "shut up!"

"Shut up!" he repeated, "or I'll terminate you on the spot! I pay Nick! I pay him! WITH MY MONEY! Who the hell told you to execute the order I gave him and him alone?!"

"He did," Laurie replied.

"And who the hell is Nick to delegate an assignment to you?! And who the hell are you to disregard my commands? I PAY HIM! And if he doesn't do his work, what the hell am I? A charity institution? A mercy home?! A welfare state?! The little nuns of the hardscrabbles?! Is that what you think I am?

Now get the hell out of my office and do the work that's assigned to you and YOU only!"

"Never ever have I put up with this sort of thing, Mr. Carbone. Never ever have I had to listen to this foul language!" Laurie had the whisper of someone trying to stay under control.

"Run along, honey, now run along!" Carbone said. "I I I have work to do."

"And for your information, Mr. Carbone, you won't have to terminate me. Tomorrow's my last day. I'll just take my paycheck and go."

"Whawhawhawhy?" Carbone asked, a bit perplexed. "You you you're not happy with us??"

"You cannot be for real," again she whispered, then walked out of his office, in full control.

"Whawhawhat's the matter with you, honey?" Carbone asked, when she was already gone.

Back in the relative safety of her own office, Laurie sat behind her desk, slipped a sheet of paper in the antique electric typewriter, and began writing her letter of resignation. Each time a tear ran down her cheek, she'd wipe it off, discreetly, then look furtively around her, hoping that nobody had noticed she was crying. But nothing ever escaped Don Gume's gossipy eye. And once he knew, everybody else knew, for he resembled a chorus in an ancient Greek play, always telling the audience what's really happening. Little by little, and one by one, Laurie's co-workers stopped fanning themselves with either manila envelopes or notepads and gathered round her. Then they asked her, with true concern in their voice, what the matter was. "I'm quitting," Laurie said, weeping a little and trying to hold back other tears. "This is a madhouse. I've never seen anything like this in my life. Besides, it's too hot in here!"

"Oh, please don't quit!" Silviana begged.

"We love you already," Don Gume added. "And Carbone, too, he love you. He is happy with you."

"You're the only serious person he's ever hired," declared Gustavo.

"You could really make a difference here," Dave commented. "Besides, you remind him of Cristina."

"Oh, please don't quit!" again, Silviana begged.

Laurie put her face in her hands and wept.

"You want I get you soda?" asked Don Gume with a
tremor of emotion in his voice. "Is no good to cry and sweat
without drinking liquid. I go get you soda. I come back right
now."

By the time Don Gume came back with three cans of soda
to compensate for all the liquid that had been lost with the
weeping, Laurie had calmed down and was fanning herself
with a notepad like everybody else. "Thank you, Mr. Gumee,"
she said when he handed her the cans and the straws and the
napkins. "You're really a very nice person," she added. But
her mind was made up. Tomorrow she'd hand in her letter of
resignation.

They were still gathered around Laurie when Carbone's
new swivel-tilter armchair arrived. Silviana rolled it down the
plastic carpet all the way to his office. "Ho! Ho!" Carbone guffawed. Minutes later, he decided to give his old eviscerated
chair to Don Gonzalo who, in turn, bequeathed his to Don
Gume who, in turn, rolled his limping, wobbly one all the way
to the stock room.

Dave spent the whole afternoon with his shoes off,
anointing the wood paneling with a brownish, smelly substance. Don Prudencio, the security guard, scrubbed the rug
with a white foam. It left rings everywhere. Laurie helped
Don Gume and Silviana roll the plastic carpet up and also
helped them roll it back out ten minutes later, for Carbone
thought that the hallway looked too bare without it.

All the broken furniture was shoved into the stock room,
to be taken back out the minute the man from Purple left. In
the middle of all this, the new account executive that Carbone
had hired showed up, and Carbone ordered Dave and Gustavo
to fill him in on Carbone & Associates, "number one in Spanish Advertising, Marketing, and Public Relations. Ho! Ho!"
Carbone guffawed. The three men stepped into the conference
room.

"They're either coming here to buy us out...It's in the air
right now, all the big Anglo agencies are..." Gustavo was saying to the new account executive ten minutes later. He
stopped in the middle of his sentence because Don Gume had
just decided to join them in the conference room. "They're
buying the Hispanic agencies." Gustavo whispered the end of
his sentence.

"Carbone never sell," Don Gume interrupted.

"What's up, guys?" Clare mumbled, the More dangling from his mouth. "Don't get up! Don't get up! I'm Clare Kelly, Executive Vice-President. Worked my way to the top! And let's all laugh. That's a joke! By golly aren't you hot?"

"Antonio Machado," the new account executive said. "Is the air conditioner broken or something?"

"Where is it that you see a broken air conditioner?!" Clare asked.

"Do you think the old devil would sell?" Gustavo asked Clare.

"And give up his throne?!" Clare blurted out. "This is all the old guy's got! But I'll tell you what he thinks. He thinks that Purple is so desperate to break into the Hispanic market that their chap's gonna come here tomorrow, fall on his knees, and beg him to take all the Purple accounts. That's what the old devil thinks."

"Wow! It sure is hot in here!" the new account executive said.

"And why do YOU think Purple's coming tomorrow?" Dave asked Clare.

"I ain't got the faintest, and we're all going to have to wait until tomorrow to find out," Clare replied, then lit another More and walked out.

"I have this hunch," Gustavo mumbled, "that they're coming here to look for talent."

"It's no use trying to open the windows, they're stuck," Dave told Antonio, the newcomer.

"Maybe they want security guard, too," Don Gume snickered. "The whole package deal. Hey, Don Prudencio, you go to work for Purple if they ask you? You wrong, Gustavo, Purple come here simply to look," Don Gume added, then pulled his lower eyelid down and moved his head from right to left and then from left to right. "And when they see," he continued, "they leave in one half-hour."

"You're probably right," Gustavo heaved a sigh.

V

Hearthrobs of victory usually made Carbone more despotic than usual. On Friday morning, not only had his dying son's condition gotten a little better—which made Car-

bone believe that he wasn't dying after all, thanks to all the
money he was spending at Christ Hospital—but the man from
Purple was expected at five-thirty, and to Carbone this meant
that billions of dollars worth of accounts were in the bag
already. And since his son was doing fine and there was no
urgent need to loiter at his bedside, Carbone was already sitting in the new swivel-tilter armchair in his office on Friday
morning by ten a.m.

"Clare!" he shouted.

"Yes, Frank?" Clare peeked in and asked.

"I want everybody in here!" Carbone roared, and slapped
the New Jersey Bell statement.

Silviana, Clare, and Laurie sat on the couch. Dave and
the new account executive took the pivoting armchairs. Gustavo was pouting next to the phone. And Don Gume and Don
Prudencio, in stiff tuxedos because of the Purple meeting,
were standing at the door fanning themselves with the 1959
wall calendars they had found in the stock room.

"You you you look good," Carbone said to his employees.

Clare, Dave, and Antonio wore three-piece suits. Gustavo
looked like a uniformed schoolboy and Silviana like a prom
girl, while Laurie, who was quitting that day, looked very corporate in that navy blue Anne Klein outfit from her Anglo
advertising days. She had on red lipstick and looked very
pretty with her hair up. Carbone looked at her and was just
about to smile when Dave asked if he could say something.

"Shut up, Dave!" Carbone snapped.

He suddenly forgot about how pretty Laurie was today
and started fumbling with the phone bill, trying to get all the
pages in a neat pile. But like most people who have been president for years, he was clumsy with his hands. Gustavo
seemed to have an itch inside his ear. Since this was taking so
long, Don Gume leaned against the wall. Carbone finally
found what he was looking for. He put his soft, padded index
finger on top of the list and proceeded, "Miami, four minutes,
Miami, seven minutes, Miami, fifteen minutes. Who the hell's
calling Miami, and why fifteen minutes?"

"That's Radio Siempre, Mr. Carbone," Silviana mentioned.

"And it goes on! Miami, twenty-seven minutes. Hope,
New Jersey, eight minutes. Philadelphia! twelve minutes.

Camden! eighteen minutes. Princeton, eighteen minutes. Whawhawhy the hell are we doing calling those places?"

"Those are the radio stations I called... The ones that cover southern New Jersey for the VerySweet account, you know," Gustavo uttered.

"Who the hell gave you that order, Gustavo?"

"You did, Sir."

"Thathathat's beside the point! It it it doesn't take eighteen minutes to ask for a media kit! Whawhawhy you've wasted a total of fifty-six minutes for goddamn media kits! No wonder you people don't get any work done around here! Youyouyou spend all your time yayayakking on the phone. Yak yak yak, and I pay for that! The world can be conquered in eight hours, but not if you spend eight minutes talking to a puny little radio station in Camden!"

"Frank, can I say something?"

"Shut up, Dave! And what's this?! Fire Island, three minutes! Why the hell are we calling Fire Island? Who called? Was it you? You? I'll find the culprit!" he roared. "I'll even dial this number if I have to! From now on, I don't want anybody using these phones without my permission!"

"But you're usually never here in the morning, Mr. Carbone," Silviana protested.

"Then call me at home! I I I can be reached! If I I I'm not here, I I I'm either at the hospital, at the bank, or at home! And if I catch any one of you using these phones without my consent, I'll terminate you on the spot and use physical force if I have to! Has everybody understood?!"

"Yes, Mr. Carbone," Silviana replied.

Before telling them to run along, he did comment on the Purple meeting, but just to advice them that they shouldn't neglect their other duties and devote all their time and thought to Purple since the Purple accounts were practically in already.

The rest of the afternoon was fairly quiet; Carbone had had his dose of kingly screaming and yelling for the day. But it was nevertheless Friday, the meeting with the man from Purple didn't change anything. Friday was the day Carbone doled out his yellow New Jersey Mutual Trust Company checks to anyone who came up with a sufficiently convincing alibi. This had gone on for years, and there was no reason for it to be any different this Friday. And like every Friday, there was a motley crew of people patiently waiting for alms. Carbone thrived on this, for they left their pride at home and usually started oozing in at three o'clock. The first ones were entitled to the homely green couch in the corridor. The limit was the end of the plastic carpet, out of Carbone's sight. He hated for them to observe him from a distance and make what he called "goo-goo" eyes. So the latecomers had to cluster together either in the reception area or in the front office, Laurie's and Don Gume's office. There were usually the same faces every Friday. The owner of La Plataforma newspaper, who had published a Beneficial Betting press release this week, was laying claim to fifty dollars, but would accept forty if he had to. Sergio, the *bodega* survey man, was expecting one hundred and fifty, while a carping photographer was showing Don Gume the pictures he had taken of the Grocer's Fair and calling him as witness in case Carbone decided, once again, to give him only twenty dollars for twenty photos. There was also a dark-skinned Dominican girl dressed in Vodoo white, supposedly the new typist, who had come in four days late, but who was now waiting for an assignment.

By five o'clock they were all gone. Carbone had been fairly generous that Friday. He also paid his staff on time, for once, but did warn them that they had to stay at the office until the meeting with Purple was over, a meeting which could take forever, which could take till nine.

The man from Purple arrived early, at quarter past five instead of five-thirty. He shook the hand of every single well-dressed member Carbone's staff and wiped the beads of sweat off his brow. Carbone then escorted him into his office and shut the door. Everyone except Don Gume and Laurie tried to eavesdrop.

Twenty minutes later, the eavesdroppers suddenly realized it was time to disperse, for Carbone and the man from Purple were both getting up and bidding each other farewell. After having arrived early, the man from Purple left early. Nobody got a chance to give him a resumé or a calling card, and Carbone merely got to say "we're number one" three times. The man from Purple said he had a plane to catch. Gustavo said, "What a bummer!" Antonio, the new chap, said, "This is real bad luck!" Clare said, "That's the way it goes!" Dave said, "Have a nice weekend, you all." Silviana said, "Everything's not lost. Mr. Carbone said the man from Purple would get back to us." Don Gonzalo said, "That's what you get for letting your personal life interfere with your . . ." Everyone said, "It was nice working with you, Laurie. Sorry to see you go."

"Any last minute gossip?" Laurie asked Don Gume when everyone was gone.

"Not today, *niña*, not today," he replied. "Oh, I'm sorry about the smoke."

"Oh, no, don't put that out, you can smoke. Finally, it doesn't bother me. Or I'm not allergic. Mr. Gumee, please light your cigarette. It really doesn't bother me, I swear. I kind of like it. Oh, my God, what am I saying?! Well, I guess I better go give my letter to Mr. Carbone and then run along!"

Past the water cooler, down the plastic carpet, past Silviana's empty desk. "May I come in for a minute, Mr. Carbone? I just wanted to give you this and tell you that I learned a lot this week. Well, I guess..."

"Whawhawhat's this?" Carbone asked, fumbling with the envelope.

"It's my letter of resignation. I guess there's just not enough of a future for me here . . ."

"Dddon't give me any of that future crcrcrnnnonsense. You're not happy here, honey, or whawhawhat? Is it the pppay? Whawhawhat is it?"

"No, it's not the pay. Actually, you pay better than the big agencies . . ."

"I do?" asked Carbone, reachng toward his pocket as if his wallet were gone.

"It's that, if I stayed here for a while, I think I'd never leave, I'd just want to stick around, and I think I'd both hate and love you too much to quit! Like your staff here. And you know what's funny, too? On Monday and Tuesday, I thought I hated it here, and that I hated the people here as well as everything about this place. Then all of a sudden, I realized that everybody was very affectionate. So my attitude changed! My attitude's changed forever! I feel so lightweight! But I want something more corporate, Mr. Carbone. I want to work in a corporate atmosphere."

"Well, honey, if you must go, I I I'm not going to be the one to keep you. Ppput whawhawhatever you want on your resumé. You you you can say you you you've worked here as

an account executive for two, three, four, five years, we're a
prestigious agency, they can call me, and I I I'll back you up!"

"A week's quite enough, Mr. Carbone. But thank you for
the thought. If ever I see your ad in the paper, I'll miss you
and everybody else here. Even the building! I have to admit
that it had this old-world charm. You know, this building.
Should I close your door?"

"Huh?! The door? No. Leave it open, honey. Will you leave
it open?"

After she left Carbone turned to the drummer bear and
fumbled with the "on" switch with his padded index finger
until he succeeded in activating it. With a wide, wrinkled,
teethless smile on his face he watched it play. "Ho-ho! Look at
its paws! Cutest thing in the world!" A little man with white
hair marveling at the drummer bear. "Don Gume!" he suddenly roared. "Ppput your jacket on! We're going to Manhattan. To fffind Cristina, my daughter. I love her. And I want
her to take over...I I I think I've lost my touch." Then he
turned to the drummer bear and added, "She she she'll probably want to remodel the office...The building?! Put in central
air conditioning?! Goddammit, I've worked all my life without
it! Fix the windows?! If something doesn't need fixing, why
why why the hell fix it?! Electric bill's gogogoing to kill me.
Sky high this year. And who does New Jersey Bell think I I I
am? The goose with the golden eggs? Will you complain about
the electric bill, Don Gume? Will you do that for me? And you
you you'll advise Cristina to be frugal, won't you, Don Gume?
If I get another one of those bills...sky-high...going to kill
me...they're all after my money...I know, Don Gume, I'm getting old. The the the batteries are low." The drummer bear
played slower and slower. Until it stopped.

GRANDMOTHER'S SECRET

Two older women were standing on the corner of Palisade and Bowers, staring at the New York City skyline in the distance. Behind them, the red letters on the glass storefront read <<Delfina's Laundry>>. Nilda Machado was fanning herself with a Catholic wall calendar. Delfina Bos was carrying a thirty-pound toddler. He was sound asleep. His feet went down to her knees. In her arms he seemed too heavy, too big.

"Poor little guy!" whispered Nilda.

"Don't worry about this child," replied Delfina. "He has a great life."

"Maybe now, but what's going to happen later when he finds out?" insinuated Nilda.

"I've been wondering about that," Delfina replied.

Just then a pregnant woman walked out of the laundromat and asked about the sweat shop across the street. Had immigration really paid them an untimely visit?

"On Wednesday," said Delfina, "and it's been shut ever since."

And had Delfina heard about the fire on Summit Avenue? Apparently, it was arson. And she also needed change, five-dollars worth. Delfina managed to pull all those quarters out of her pocket without disturbing the child who continued sleeping soundly in her arms.

"But I'll never talk to your daughter for as long as I live," confessed Nilda after the pregnant woman had gone back into the laundromat. "Not even hello, how are you? Not after what she did to my son."

Just to make her point, Nilda added that even God wasn't obliged to forgive everything. Even Jesus Christ got mad once! A girl shouldn't behave the way that Sylvia did, especially not with poor Antonio who had always treated her so well. That was unforgivable! They had fallen in love when they were both sixteen, and during the two years that followed, poor Tonio bought her presents and took her to the movies and the restaurant and they made all these plans to study medicine and then get married. And poor Tonito had always respected Sylvia, and Sylvia herself was always telling everyone, well not everyone, that Tonio was the love of her life. Was she just being a hypocrite? Then she got accepted into Cornell University, and poor Tonito was really happy for her, and they threw a party to celebrate. Remember the party, Delfina? Remember the party? The pig they roasted, the music, the laughter, the fried bananas. So why did Sylvia do that? Hadn't poor Antonito been humiliated enough, especially after having been denied a grant by every single university in the world? That because he was madly in love with her, and things like that distract men...He'd even gotten a part-time job while he was in high school, poor thing, in order to buy Sylvia presents and take her out to the restaurant. Because that was back when Sylvia had little or no appetite when she was sitting at a kitchen table but could really eat when she was in a restaurant. A Latin princess, that's what she was! And princesses don't need to get part-time jobs when they're in high school. She had all that extra time to study. Then in September, she left for Cornell, and Tonito, poor thing, had to join the North Carolina army so they'd pay for his studies. What kind of contrast is that? But that wasn't enough! Eight months later Sylvia returns from Cornell and tells everyone she's pregnant! Couldn't she have been more discreet about it? She practically had it published in the newspaper. Sylvia Bos is pregnant and unmarried, and she swears that this is not Antonio Machado's child. He's never even touched her, and she's proud and happy to be carrying a a a...bastard!

A man with lots of gold jewelry and a huge scar under his eye came to ask for liquid soap. So Delfina pulled a set of keys out of her pocket and said she had to get some in the back, but that it would take a while since she might as well leave the baby upstairs with her daughter Yolanda.

Inside the laundromat, at that moment, there was so much talk of immigration officials and of fake Social Security cards that the words seemed to have the scent of April fresh fabric softener. For several minutes, Nilda stood there listening. As usual she didn't want to miss any of it. But this time, standing there, arms crossed and forehead wrinkled up, she was determined not to join any of these conversations. Delfina would be back any minute now, and maybe she would finally tell her who the child's father was. What if she got stuck with another illegal alien's life story? But for Nilda, to refrain from voicing her opinions was as difficult as not breathing. So she finally blurted out, to all those present, so she wouldn't get stuck with any individual, that she herself was happy to be Cuban and to have an American passport, because the Americans were really getting tough with the illegals these days. She then lost her train of thought and wondered out loud why in the world it was so hot today. But she soon remembered what she was talking about and warned a woman from Nicaragua about those lawyers who say they can get you your papers when in fact all they want to do is squeeze the last penny out of you. And then they run off with your money. It happens every single day.

When Delfina returned, they were debating on which country had the most majestic Cathedrals. "Lord Jesus Christ, what's happening with the weather?!" exclaimed Nilda, who was quickly bored by the talk of cathedrals. Nilda was a reputed doomsayer, and indeed, the minute she couldn't get her word in about impending doom, she was totally bored with the conversation. But they carried on with this talk of cathedrals. Delfina voted for the Dominican Republic, not that she'd ever been there, but according to her daughter Sylvia, who had studied medicine in Santo Domingo ("After having failed at Cornell," interrupted Nilda.), Santo Domingo had the most incredible cathedrals you could imagine.

"They'll never find a cure for cancer!" Nilda said to a lady from Peru.

Then a woman from Tenosique asked Delfina if any sweat shops were hiring in the neighborhood. Delfina advised her to keep her baby-sitting job. "In the sweat shops they treat you like dirt," she said.

"But you make good money and lots of friends," argued the woman from Tenosique.

"But immigration can pay you a visit any time, and before you know it you're deported," interrupted Nilda, who had just gotten exasperated because the Peruvian woman insisted that there was a cure for cancer.

"Stay where you are," Delfina urged the woman from Tenosique. "O.K.?" Finally the woman from Tenosique seemed convinced. That's the way it always was with Delfina.

People came from a ten-block radius to ask Delfina for advice. She knew what doctors to send people to for this or for that, and what lawyer, and what travel agent, and what accountant, and what insurance agent. She knew Jersey City by heart, because she had lived there for twenty-six years, twenty of which had been spent on this corner of Palisade Avenue. She and her husband had bought this property twenty years ago when property in this area was dirt cheap because hardly anybody dared to live here.

The laundromat had its cycles, and suddenly it became calm. These were the times when, weather permitting, Delfina would stand outside the laundromat and either gossip with the passers-by, or warn the sixteen-years-olds that she'd known since before they were born that if she caught them dealing crack around here...Or shout at the traffic cops for not being fair, only putting tickets on the cars they'd never seen. Or simply stand there watching the children playing on the sidewalk, the people crossing the street, the cars honking, the buses stopping, letting passengers out, quietly watching over everything, like the mother-goddess of the neighborhood that she was.

Nilda Machado went to join Delfina outside. Nilda swore that the earth was inching its way toward the sun. If not it wouldn't be this hot.

"And I don't have anything against you, you know that," said Nilda, still fanning herself with the Catholic wall calendar. "Did you ever find out who the father was?"

"Remember how sick I got three years ago, Nilda?"

"Of course you got sick! What else can you expect when you're paying all that money to send your daughter to Cornell University so she can come out a doctor, and it turns out that instead of becoming a doctor she ends up needing a doctor because she's pregnant? At least she had the decency of having the baby in Miami instead of here in Jersey City because that would've really killed my poor Tonito." Nilda kept on talking and fanning herself at full speed. Then she reminded Delfina about how sick she got when that stray bullet she had for a daughter told her she was expecting. Delfina was so upset that she couldn't keep anything down. Did Delfina remember that? Little does it matter whether Delfina remembers. Nilda remembers. Nilda remembers everything. She says she has the best of memories. Every ten minutes or so Delfina would rush to the bathroom and vomit. She just couldn't keep anything down. The whole neighborhood remembers that. Everybody guessed that she had gotten cancer of the stomach because of the grief and gave her approximately six months to live.

"Me, too. First I thought it was because of the menopause, then I thought I had cancer," Delfina said.

And her condition kept getting worse and worse, and it didn't help any to have that daughter of hers suddenly announce that she was pregnant and even seem proud of it.

"Well, she didn't say she was pregnant right away," Delfina said. "First she came home because she was worried about me. I was very sick."

"Then a month later, just when you're beginning to feel a little better, she gives you this bombshell of news about being pregnant."

"And two weeks after that, we left for Miami," Delfina added. "I don't know what came over me. I was so embarrassed! It was Sylvita's fault. She was even more embarrassed than I was. Embarrassment is contagious, you know."

"She sure didn't seem embarrassed!" Nilda commented. "So, who's the father?! The child's two years old! You're my best friend and I have the right to know!"

"But it's a secret!" Delfina chuckled.

Sylvia was so embarrassed that she didn't even want Delfina to tell the others. Yolandita was in ninth grade, and Sylvia strictly forbade Delfina to tell Yolandita. She said she didn't want her sister to be traumatized. She was much too young to hear something like that. As to Carlos, his wife was pregnant, which meant that Delfina was about to become a grandmother. He had to be spared. So did Teresita, because she had just married a man of a much higher social class. And Eduardito had this sense of the family, and he wouldn't believe his ears if anybody told him. Why, he'd have a fit! He'd be embarrassed to tears! But Delfina was adamant. Her other children should know what was going on. This was a family matter. And once the whole family knew, Delfina left for Miami with Sylvia and Big Bos, her husband.

"That was the best decision you ever made in your life, Delfina. Closing the laundromat for six months, then going to hide your shame in Miami. It's really too bad that that daughter of yours missed the rest of the year at Cornell, isn't it? Especially after your having spent all that money to send her there. It makes you wonder what the world is coming to these days."

A New Jersey Transit bus stopped right in front of them, opened its doors, let some passengers out, and waited for the green light. Delfina was telling Nilda that Sylvita didn't spend all that time in Miami. She returned to Cornell and continued studying until the baby was due. That's when she returned to Miami.

"Then that daughter of yours went back to Cornell and left you with the baby," Nilda reminded her. "Then she decides to marry someone who wasn't even the father and starts to get failing grades at Cornell. I really don't know what's wrong with girls these days. No principles, no morals, no responsibility. What's the world coming to? And you'll see, Delfina, one of these days Yolanda'll probably get pregnant. If this happened once, it can happen again. And don't say that I didn't warn you!"

"No. I don't think this could happen again," Delfina chuckled. "Anyway, let me do the talking. Three years ago I thought that it was all over. You know what I mean, the menopause. Well, I guess you wouldn't know since they emptied you so long ago. Anyway, as you already know, my daughter Sylvia was studying medicine at Cornell, and my other daughter, Yolandita, was in ninth grade, and my son Carlos was about to become a father, and my daughter Teresita had married into wealth and prestige, and my other son, Eduardo, thought I was the Virgin Mary...I really wonder why my children reacted the way they did. No, I don't. We gave them a good education, so they began to think they were superior, that's all!"

"Superior!" exclaimed Nilda. "You call a woman who brings a bastard into this world superior?!"

But Delfina hasn't finished with her story. And she's still saying "hola!" to all the passers-by she knows by name and personal fate, and the New Jersey Transit Buses are still letting people out right there on that street corner. Three years ago, Delfina suddenly began to feel very sick, and first she thought it was because of the menopause, and then she thought it was stomach cancer, and Big Bos, her husband, was so worried that he took her to Christ Hospital one Friday afternoon to have a sonogram and at least know the truth. The nurse put this jelly on her stomach, and the doctor had this little machine that looks like a radar detector. He passed it over her belly. You could see her insides on a screen. Big Bos had tears in his eyes. He was expecting a tumor the size of a grapefruit. Suddenly they saw a little thing floating around in her insides. That's when Big Bos started jumping up and down with joy. Delfina couldn't believe her eyes. She thought she knew what it was.

But more disconcerting was Big Bos' reaction. Why was he so happy? This was an unexpected catastrophe. He even started shouting "hurray! hurray hurray!" He ran over to her and kissed her and hugged her and said, "You only have worms!"

And the nurse, who was Puerto Rican, said, "Hey, Granpa, that sure ain't no worm!"

But Big Bos kept insisting. He was shouting, "Parasites! Parasites! A solitary worm! That's no cancer!"

Finally, the doctor went over to shake his hand and congratulate him. Big Bos was going to be a father! When he heard this, Big Bos stopped jumping up and down, and his jaw went all the way down to his belly button. Then he turned to Delfina and said, "Have you no shame?! And just about to become a grandmother? And at your age? Fifty-one and pregnant like an eighteen-year-old? Are you trying to compete with your daughter-in-law? What happened? What is this?" Delfina and Big Bos had this shouting match right there in front of the doctor and the nurse who didn't quite know what to say. Half-an-hour later the yells and screams subsided. Delfina and Big Bos turned to the doctor and asked, "What should we tell the children? They'll kill us!"

Back home, Sylvia was eagerly expecting their arrival. The minute they opened the door she ran to them and asked what the matter was, was it nothing? was it cancer? That's when she saw tears in both Delfina's and Big Bos' eyes and began shouting, "Oh, my God! Oh, my God! It's cancer! Oh, my God, why is this happening to us?" She was hysterical, she just couldn't stop crying, so her father decided to tell her the truth right then and there just to calm her down. But instead of having its desired effect, the news of her mother's pregnancy only made things worse. For a while it seemed as if cancer would've been a more honorable fate.

Sylvia shouted, "I'll die of shame! I'll never be able to go out in the street with this old lady parading a pregnant belly in front of her!" Then she couldn't believe it. There must be an error. How could somebody Delfina's age be pregnant? Impossible! They were both too old. Besides, nobody was going to tell Sylvia that her parents, her parents, of all people.... It was absolutely impossible. Anyway, doctors made mistakes all the time.

"You mean you saw it?!" Sylvia yelled. "On the screen? You had a sonogram? Oh, my God, this is crazy. This is crazy. This is the craziest thing I've ever heard in my life! Mami, don't you know about birth control? Or just about control in general? Weren't you the first one to tell me that only ignorant girls got pregnant? Doesn't that include old ladies? What is this, a circus? A freak show? Besides, isn't five children enough?"

She just couldn't believe it. "I'm freaking out," she said. Her father told her to speak Spanish, no English allowed in the house. Then she said something about having had to abide by their rules when they didn't have any themselves. What would her brothers say? "They'll kill, Daddy! Daddy, they'll think you raped her!" What would the tenants think! It was flagrant! They couldn't say it just happened by osmosis! And poor Antonio, her boyfriend, what would he say? "Like mother, like daughter," probably. He was going to think she had a loose mother! What would the neighbors say? What would the neighborhood think? And Jersey City? And New Jersey? And the world! And the people at Cornell? Her mother practically in the Guiness Book of World Records!

"Mami, I've never been so embarrassed in my whole life!" Sylvia yelled. "Congratulations, you've just ruined my existence!"

The other four children didn't have a much better reaction. Yolandita threatened to commit suicide and asked her mother to put herself in her place. "Mami, how would you feel if I got pregnant all of a sudden?" As to Carlos, his first reaction was a "who did this?" reaction, but he didn't go that far. Then he turned to his father and was just about to say something, but kept quiet. Then he said, "Is this, or is this not grotesque?" Then he wondered what he was going to tell his unborn child. That his uncle or his aunt or whatever that thing turned out to be was younger than he was? Might as well not tell them anything. This was a family scandal and all scandals should be kept quiet.

Of the five children, it was Eduardo who had the worst reaction. He went as far as comparing his parents to Adam and Eve! And his nephew was going to have Adam and Eve for grandparents! "Just another Hispanic statistic," Eduardo said sarcastically. "Five and a half children per household. We could be the model Hispanic family! Bravo! Can't stop having children until we die! We'll populate the whole United States of America!"

"Speak Spanish," Big Bos said. "No English in the house."

Eduardo had been working in his uncle's Hispanic advertising agency, and the somewhat racist census bureau facts concerning Hispanics seemed to have deeply affected him, as an Hispanic. "We're number one in everything!" he complained.

"Speak Spanish, Eduardo!" his father commanded.

"I'd rather forget Spanish!' Eduardo retorted. "And my name's Ed!"

"Ed! Ed! Go to hell with your Ed! I named you Eduardo! You'll always be Eduardito in this family!" Big Bos started shouting. "And it's because you were bi-cultural that you got your job! It's because you belonged to a minority that the university gave you a grant! And now you want to belong to the majority! You want to be Irish!"

"A hell of a lot you know about minority groups!" Eduardo retorted.

"Speak Spanish."

"You know as much about minorities as you know about birth control. But that's beside the point; this is way over your head, Dad. I realize you both like to play Adam and Eve, but I hope you realize that, this,…that, even for high-risk pregnancies you're over the hill…The statistics say that high-risk pregnancies are from thirty-five to forty-five…I guess most of the statistics assume that women calm down after that age…They didn't take my mother into consideration. Ten years ago this would've been a high-risk pregnancy. Doesn't that make you stop and wonder what it is now?"

"Maybe it reverts to low-risk," Delfina said.

"Mami, you've done your share, no joking now, O.K?"

He kept on talking about Adam and Eve and saying that, compared to his parents, they were probably absolved now. All Eve had done was eat an apple. Then he wanted to talk about abortion, but his parents refused to hear about it. "Would you have wanted us to abort you?" Big Bos asked his son.

"Don't get me into this," Eduardo replied. "I have nothing to do with this."

This family drama took place in Delfina's and Big Bos' kitchen. And it continued through the night. A vicious circle of conversation that Big Bos didn't even participate in anymore. Suddenly, it seemed to have dawned on him that he was going to be a father for the sixth time, and he seemed proud of himself, he seemed happy! Whenever one of his children told him about how old he was, he replied, "Me? Old? Ha!" then chuckled by himself in his corner. Sylvita and Yolandita were weeping with their heads in their hands, Teresita was wondering what her husband would think, and would this ruin her marriage, and Big Bos said, "This is the first time we won't have to worry about how we're going to support the child."

"The freak, you mean," Eduardo corrected him. "It's in the statistics. There's over a hundred percent chance that he'll be a mongolian freak."

"If we're both Cuban, how can he be Mongolian?" Delfina asked.

"Mami, please, you've done your share. No jokes, O.K?"

"Mami," Sylvita interrupted. "I study medicine. I'm into science. So at least listen to me. That won't necessarily be a baby like us . . ."

"Thank God!' Big Bos said. "Me? Old? Ha! Mongolian! Ha-ha! Maybe he'll be Irish! Ha-ha-ha! We've lived in this country long enough!"

"The Irish are not the majority in this country, for your information," Eduardo said.

"He could even have a pig's tail! Yuk!" Yolandita said. "I read that in a novel."

"Speak Spanish," Bis Bos said.

"I don't know how to express myself in Spanish!"

"Don't know how to express yourself in English either," her father said.

"I have a solution," Sylvia said.

At first, Delfina and Big Bos didn't even want to hear this; they said it was out of the question. But, little by little, their children convinced them. In fact, they convinced them that they would be ridiculous. They'd be the laughing stock of the neighborhood. So it was agreed that Sylvia would take her mother's "shameful" place. The next day, she'd start telling everyone that she was pregnant. And the rest would be easy. She'd go back to Cornell; her mother would go to Miami, have the baby, and if the baby survived, she'd come back here and say it was Sylvia's. It was even better for the baby. Wouldn't he be ashamed of having such old parents? Didn't Delfina and Big Bos know by now how children were? Or had they forgotten? Children want to be like everybody else. They don't want to be original. They don't want to be singled out. And the little thing she was carrying would certainly be singled out if it had such old parents.

"It'll probably die anyway," Eduardo said. "It's in the statistics. A leftover egg. It can't survive. Anyway, it's an utter lack of responsibility..."

"You teach your children about responsibility and then it's the boomerang,"

Big Bos interrupted. "Me? Old? Ha!"

❋　❋　❋

Another New Jersey Transit bus stopped to let some passengers out. For the first time in her life Nilda was silent. She wanted to say a thousand things at the same time, but nothing came out. She coughed. She was aghast. She stuck the wall calendar under her arm and desperately searched for a tissue in her pocketbook and blew her nose. She was almost choking. Nothing would come out. She was back to fanning herself wildly. She finally managed to ask, "Delfina, how did it happen?"

"So anyway," Delfina said. "In order to keep our children happy and spare Little Bos the shame of having grandparents for parents, hola! we both agreed to put on this show. But he's mine, Nilda. He's mine."

Paloma

Her land was green and brown, and rolling and grooved by torrents. It rained almost all year long. It rained harder in September, October, November. It was a tropical rain. It gorged the air and the earth. It made the ground swell. Her village was Indian, Mauresque, Spanish, as colorful, as busy, as warm as a Peruvian blanket. There was an old yellow Cathedral, a market place, a flower square. There were several parks staked with statues erected in honor of Spanish heroes some of which were now buried in the graveyard adjacent to the church, a tourist attraction. The oldest headstone was from 1518, but the name was impossible to read; the constant rain had made the stone melt. On some of the other headstones Spanish names such as Grijalva, Jaramillo, and Torquemada could be deciphered; names respected and renowned for having imported to the New World the Medieval mysticism, the self-punishment, and the humble submission that her people, because of their wise inborn serenity and survival instinct, had accepted from the very beginning. They hardly had enough to eat, but that was God's will; their ancestors too had lived and survived on half-empty stomachs; they even got fat. There was corruption everywhere, but it was so common that it was confused with normality. Those who weren't satisfied with the system escaped to that paradise called the United States instead of complaining or fighting or trying to alter the deeply rooted ways. They'd been taught that any effort here wasn't really worth making. They'd best save their energy and willpower for America. In truth, corruption was so bad that, in terms of money, it took several years of hard labor. For those who had no connections to obtain something as simple as a passport. So the luckier ones who held this precious document didn't even travel. They stayed where they were and took good advantage of their passports. But, whether lucky or unlucky, instead of trying to

climb mountains, her people did the best they could to make
their way around the mountains.

Paloma Sánchez stood five feet two inches on her bare
feet. She was a tiny little thing with shoulder-length black
hair that was curly because of semi-annual permanent waves.
From the time they were twelve or thirteen, the women from
her village resorted to this kind of hair treatment; their hair
was too straight if left natural, and they didn't seem to like it
natural. Paloma's skin was ripe olive. She was lean and mus-
cular. Her teeth were shiny white and perfect. She had black
almond-shaped eyes and a little-bird quality to her demeanor.
And she was pretty. Extremely so. So pretty that a boy of fifteen had claimed her when she was thirteen, and they were
married in haste a month later. But that was normal, about
as normal as not being able to obtain a passport without
money or connections. Even the homely ones married young,
life was so hard that they did everything quickly, perhaps just
to be done with it.

But Paloma wasn't normal. She was among the luckier
ones in that at age twenty-five, when she went to the market
place with her ten, eleven and twelve-year-old sons, she still
made heads turn; men thought these boys were her brothers.
She hadn't aged quickly like most of the other women.
Rodrigo, her husband, always bragged about having married
the most beautiful woman in this land. And Rodrigo was the
one who came up with the bad idea of having Paloma's picture taken.

If the sleeping dogs had been left to lie, maybe Paloma
wouldn't have gone to prison and hers would have been a normal life.

But to commemorate every special occasion in their lives,
Rodrigo insisted on dragging Paloma to a little photo studio in
the village. At first Paloma didn't want to; she was scared of
x-rays and cameras. And the more she went, the more she
was humiliated and terrified now. Rodrigo quickly took to
repeating the same exact thing after the flash had gone off
and Paloma's image had been gulped by the camera. With a
loud sigh of relief he'd say that (at last!) her children and
future grandchildren would realize how beautiful she had
once been. He'd also add that it'd be different this time, that
she'd come out looking as spectacular as she was, technology
was advancing, practically every day progress was being

made with flashes and cameras. Paloma needn't worry. This time she wouldn't be offended by the developed photograph. She'd have a photo she was proud of! This never happened.

These humiliating photo sessions began when Paloma was eighteen. It was in honor of their fifth wedding anniversary. Paloma had already borne three children then, but she had also managed to graduate from high school thanks to the help and cooperation she got from her parents and immediate family. Rodrigo, too, had graduated from high school and they both had excellent jobs. Paloma stayed in her village and worked as a secretary in the administration. Rodrigo was a customs official in the capital. They only saw each other once a month; but this way of life allowed them luxuries such as photo sessions for Christmas, birthdays and anniversaries, meat or fowl every night on their table, decent clothes, a decent dwelling. The clothes were extremely important for Paloma; she was a gentle, sensitive woman with a little vain streak, it happens even to the gentle and the sensitive—and this is precisely why the photo sessions made her life take a turn that nobody had expected.

Neither Paloma nor Rodrigo were disappointed at first. They laughed and blamed it on the flash. So did they the second time. Then it was the photographer. Then it was the camera. Then it was because she was pregnant for the fourth time. They also tried to blame it on the rain. After that, it was her nerves—everybody gets nervous on special occasions. They tried July, that run-of-the-mill month July, when nothing was happening. Still no good. They finally went to the capital. Photographers in the capital were far more competent; they were sure they wouldn't be disappointed.

But they obtained the same puzzling results and this time Paloma overreacted. She cried and swore that she'd never have her picture taken again. She even wondered if she was as ugly as she appeared on a developed photograph. She sobbed and complained that life wasn't worth living if her—she didn't say "beauty"—if her good looks were to disappear one day without leaving a trace. Her perplexed husband tried to comfort her. It was difficult though, for he himself was disappointed, he just couldn't understand. How was it that he had married the most beautiful woman in this land and that she was so homely on a developed photograph? He always bragged about her to his buddies in the airport and had, time after time, promised to bring them a photo of her. But he just couldn't get round to it! How could he show them the image of a common-looking matron after years of bragging?! They'd tell him that love was certainly blind! Rodrigo still had to comfort his wife though, so he put his wounded pride to one side. It wasn't that she actually looked ugly…it was…What was it? It was that she looked like anybody else. Common! Paloma sobbed even harder. Rodrigo's wife, Paloma. Paloma of all people! Paloma looked common on a photograph! Even the photographer couldn't understand what had happened. He argued that he usually made women looked prettier than they really were. He even insisted on taking several other pictures of Paloma who finally gave in after having chanted and chanted "never again" at least fifty times. But the same exact results were obtained again and again. She was as pretty as a bird, but on a photo she looked like anyone. Like everyone. From that day on, Paloma and Rodrigo acted as if she were afflicted by some unknown disease that no doctor could diagnose. For a while they continued running from doctor to doctor, still no result.

One day, Paloma finally dried her tears and said with the resolution of wounded pride, "so be it!" If she was condemned to lose her good looks, if in twenty year's time she wouldn't even be able to produce paper proof of her youth, well, then, she'd start living. Wasn't she, after all, dissatisfied with her life? She'd married too young and that thrill was gone. She had children and she was a loving mother, but the children just couldn't fill the void. What exactly awaited her? More Christmases. More wedding anniversaries. More birthdays. Her children would grow up and marry, and she'd most likely be a grandmother before age thirty, then a great grandmother at forty-five. Then what? She'd wither and die.

Paloma was born strange. She had always wondered about the meaning of life. She was born dissatisfied. Since puberty she had tried to dilute this unpleasure and swallow it. Like a ghost, it always returned to its haunted house. So if a dull fate was the only thing in store for her, Paloma, who was five feet two inches tall, decided once and for all to walk around it.

She was going to put fine clothes and jewels on her body. She'd have many loves. She'd know the pangs of passion as many times as her spirit could take them without breaking.

She'd be married to many, many men. She'd live in sixty different places at the same time. Perhaps she wasn't photogenic. So be it, she'd make the best of it. She knew how to do
it. It was a rusty, broken old gift that she'd left behind. At
puberty. When she got married and had convinced herself
that it was just child's play. Back then it had seemed more
important to become an adult, bear children, celebrate Christmas with the family, show your children off, the cute things
they say and do, hide behind them, die progressively behind
them, give up, be serious. Now she was determined to bring
the child Paloma back.

She asked the local photographer to take a small picture
of her, the kind you use for passports. A week later, when she
went to pick her photo I.D.'s up, the photographer, who knew
her well, said, "I think I could sell that exact same photo to
any woman who walks in here." Paloma smiled and said, "I
know that."

Because she worked in the administration and Rodrigo
was a customs official, both she and her husband had certain
privileges that the majority of her people wouldn't even
dream about. In three months she had her passport. Rodrigo,
who was more than content and even proud of his fate, said,
"We're not leaving. We're not going to New York." It was
absolutely out of the question. Their people suffered there.
"Besides, our whole family's here. And the children need their
cousins to play with. And Christmas wouldn't be Christmas..."
Paloma interrupted him, she said, "Don't worry, I'm staying
right here."

Christmas came and went. It barely gave them enough
time to try again at the photo studio, to obtain the same offensive results, and to roast a pig at the routine family reunion.
Paloma became distant and aloof. Everything saddened her;
the food, the festivities, the gifts, the family. She wanted to
cry, she wanted to die. The evil depression was gnawing away
at her spirit. She tried to cheer up. It was to no avail. Her
black eyes were constantly holding back the tears. What was
the use of it? One more Christmas. One more wasted year.
She was twenty-six, and she felt old and worn-out. She felt
her life slipping by, and her youth. She looked in the mirror
and noticed thin lines around her eyes. Nothing to look forward to. Nothing but this. While everyone was merry and
sentimental, thanking the Lord that they were together, she

felt like dying. She didn't consider herself a part of it. She felt
trapped. She suddenly wished her husband would leave her,
set her free. Sad heart, dirty hands. For the few days that followed she thought she was insane. Why this grief? Would it
ever leave her? Christmas was supposed to be a happy sea-
son. But why pretend? So insane she must be. She wanted to
die, that was all. Couldn't they just leave her alone?

Then came the feast of Saint Sylvester, the new year. Her
resolution was to fly, up in the sky, way up high. Yes! She'd
fly! And she'd fly before she became a grandmother. She
swore to that!

It so happened that her thirteen-year-old son had gotten
a nineteen-year-old spinster pregnant. They'd married in
haste like everybody else and the baby was due in March.
This didn't leave Paloma that much time to fly.

Three Kings Day she fell into a strange torpor. Sons and
daughters and nieces and nephews were happily opening
their presents. Children were laughing and playing and running and shouting, but Paloma saw and heard nothing. She
still remained a loving mother. She continued being the gentle creature she was. But she was just pretending to be there.
In reality, she was dreaming. Dreaming. She dreamt she was
flying.

The bird was white. It had swallowed many people. You
could see half the earth below you. The bird roared and whis-
tled. It was cold in the bird's stomach, Paloma could see its
wings of steel breaking the clouds in two. There was a woman
sitting next to her. She was small and thin, and looked just
like Paloma did on a developed photograph. And she wasn't
the only one. All the women inside the bird looked exactly like
Paloma's image on paper. "Are you scared?" the woman sitting next to her suddenly asked. Was there anything to be
afraid of? Could this bird fall? She laughed and said, "Oh, you
poor thing! The bird falling! That's the last thing in the world
to be scared of!" Because the bird will land and you have to
walk out of it. Into another world where many, many things
are magic. But it remains a hard cruel world, a bit like ours,
only different. Different because nothing's really obvious. Not
even corruption. The truth is masked. Act normal though.
Like a tourist. Tell them you're only here for two weeks to
visit your family. If you don't convince them, they'll catch you!
Don't worry about getting slapped around. They only do that

in our land. At least that's what I've been told so far. What
they do is catch you and send you back! That's when they hit
you, when you get back. And they take you by the elbow. Push
you around. You lose the freedom you never had. Have to
start over a year later when you finally get out of jail. All
those years of hard work to get papers and money to climb
into the bird...lost! Lost forever! Have to start all over again.
Aren't you scared? Of starting all over again? Yes.

The next day was a Sunday. Paloma woke up early. Her
hands were shaking. Word got to her unexpectedly. And she
knew where she had to go. She was ready. Rodrigo asked,
"Aren't we going to Mass?" Paloma didn't answer. He then
wanted her to get back into bed. That same afternoon he was
returning to the capital, they wouldn't see each other for a
month, shouldn't she get back into bed? Paloma said she
never ever wanted to be pregnant again. She slipped her
passport into her handbag and walked out of the house. She
had nothing to hide.

The bus stopped near the market place. Her destination
was an hour away. She went down, down; the hills got higher,
greener, browner, the torrents became streams. After having
stepped off the bus, she had to walk a while. The earth was
soft and the mud ankle-high. There was a woman washing
clothes in the river and crying. Her husband had had an accident. His legs were broken. He couldn't leave on Wednesday.
The money was wasted. They'd have to start all over again.
For years he'd planned this trip to New York. He was to work
there and send money home. It was terrible because they'd
begun building their house when they were newlyweds fifteen
years ago. With cement blocks. Then they ran out of cement
blocks. The next door neighbors offered to share one of their
walls, but that only gave them a house with three walls. Their
house was missing a wall. A plastic canvas had been nailed to
that empty side. It worked fine when it didn't rain. The problem was that it rained almost every day and the canvas didn't
keep the rain out.

Paloma walked downhill with her, and her house was
indeed missing a wall. The house had a door though. They
used the door. It was even locked. As if the house had four
walls. They'd saved a lot of money. It didn't take long to convince the woman's husband. They gave the money to Paloma
and Paloma gave them instructions.

She didn't go to work on Monday. With the intention of spending the newly earned money on herself, she went shopping, but ended up buying clothes and toys for her children instead. She also bought a layette for her grandchild that was due in March. By mid-afternoon the money was gone.

On Wednesday she dreamt she was flying. The bird was going down, down. Underneath her was the American city of Miami. Flat and full of lights, it looked like a gigantic amusement park. There was that same woman sitting beside her. She was afraid they'd catch her, and Paloma, too, was afraid they'd catch her. Those people in uniforms. That was their job. To catch you. They ask all kinds of questions. Even if you're telling the truth it makes you nervous. The bird landed. The stairs moved. The rubber rug moved. The suitcases moved like a serpent in the grass; you had to hurry up and catch them. Imagine your immobile suitcase passing in front of you! You wait, that's all. Then there was a line. The most dangerous part. All her people were nervous. What if they were sent back? English was a strange language. You can't understand it. But you could also hear Spanish. With a different accent. The man in the uniform wanted her passport and the yellow card that she had filled before the bird put its feet on the ground. The woman sitting next to her had had problems filling it out. She could barely read and write. The man looked at her, then at her passport, then back at her. "What's you name?" he asked. So he repeated it in Spanish. Why did he speak English if he spoke Spanish? Paloma Sánchez. Your name? Paloma Sánchez. Your name? Date of birth? March 26, 1962. Learned all that by heart. Your name? Date of birth? First time you've been here? Open your suitcase! Final destination? New York. Where? Why? Where are you coming from? How long? Why? To visit my family. How long? How much money have you got? By the way, what's your birthdate? Step to the side; some women are coming to search you and ask you your name. And ask you to sign your name several times. Paloma had never been as terrified in her life. She felt the blood gushing up to her head. She thought it would burst. How long would this last? Was it worthwhile? What's your name? Paloma Sánchez. What if they caught her? What if they sent her back? Very well. You may go. Have a nice flight. Was that it?

There were corridors and it was cold. Somebody said it was the air conditioning; nobody could live here without it. And the stairs that went up by themselves. And the rubber mat that went exactly where you were going and took you there. Gate fourteen. Was she free? When the bird landed in New York, would they ask her more questions? That woman again! Waiting to get on the other bird. Maybe she'd know. She seemed to know everything. They were both glad they didn't get caught. Then they started talking about the others. The ones who weren't waiting here with them. That meant they had gotten caught, the woman said. She loved talking about terrible things, and pitying the others.

Queens, New York. So many clothes to buy. Beautiful, beautiful stores. The people from this village of Queens are so friendly and helpful. And it's a pretty village. They sell food everywhere. Cheap. The prices don't change, apparently. When it rains, your feet don't get stuck in the mud. Queens is clean. And everybody in Queens seems to own a refrigerator. They put their clothes in machines, wait a while, then their clothes come out clean. Here you don't wash your clothes in the river. A distant cousin of hers who's been here for two years laughed when she asked where the river was. He said that the river here is much dirtier than the clothes will ever get. It's called the East River. Anyway, you can't kneel and wash your clothes in it.

A week later she had a job. They called this town Manhattan. And she kept wondering where New York City was. She wanted to visit New York City. Everybody said it was fabulous. New York City, where was it?. And until she learned the truth, she regretted having to work in Manhattan.

One hundred and fifty dollars a week. She was to cook, clean, take care of the children, speak Spanish to the children. Their mother wanted them to be bilingual. What was bilingual? Vacuum? She preferred to sweep. But the mistress was adamant. She had to push that scary machine around. What if it swallowed her? The mistress said you have to vacuum. You have to keep everything very clean. They don't want germs in their apartment. The mistress spoke some Spanish. She said she learned it in Mexico. Every morning, rain or shine, she and her husband would put sport shoes on and go running. Why do people run away from nothing? They said it was to stay in shape. Thin. So that's why the mistress looked like a skeleton. And in spite of all the money they seemed to have, they never put meat or fowl on their table. They said chicken was very, very bad for you. Imagine that! Pork was a bad word. Imagine that! Pork was supposed to be a feast. Now it's bad. Must be the pork here. They ate like rabbits. Maybe they didn't have that much money after all.... No sugar allowed either. The mistress said that sugar gave you cancer. What's cancer? Like rabbits, they ate lettuce and raw vegetables. One day they found out that she was giving their children fried food and they got very angry.

She had decided to save every penny she earned and send it home. But the girls wrote to her and said they wanted American clothes. Could she send them some? Reebok sport shoes, stretch jeans, thick socks . . . So one Saturday when she was in Queens visiting her distant relatives, she asked them to take her shopping. At first she was cautious. She only spent two hundred dollars. But the following weekend she thought that what she'd bought wasn't enough. Might as well buy more and send one big package home. It wasn't long before that was all she could think about. At night when she was lying in bed, she'd think of everything she had to buy on Saturday. The lists got longer and longer. She began needing things she never needed before. Suddenly twenty pairs of underwear weren't enough. She always needed more. And there was always that extra sweater she couldn't live without. And every time she got a new sweater she needed new pants. And the shoes to go with each new outfit. Every Saturday she ended up buying herself a new pair of shoes. There were so many shoes to buy! Then one hundred and fifty dollars weren't enough. She needed more; she needed to buy more. For the first time in her life she wanted, wanted, and suffered for wanting. Her heart ached when her eyes explored that last store window, and her arms were heavy with packages. She'd already spent all her salary. And that last pair of pants there, she wanted them! She began living for Saturday afternoon. That was all she could think about.

Paloma quit her job in the administration. She said she was too tired. With a sarcastic grin on their lips, her brothers, sisters, cousins, aunts, uncles, and even mother and father wondered why in the world she was so tired. After all, she hardly ever did anything in the house. Her daughter-in-law took care of that. The young girl cooked, cleaned, washed dishes, laundered, took care of the children, and gossiped about how Paloma spent her days either staring into blank space, or talking to herself, or telling the youngest children the weirdest stories, supposedly her adventures in America. Lies, all lies! One day her daughter-in-law asked her why she lied like that. Why tell the children stories of stairs that go upstairs by themselves? Why in the world make up stories when there were so many other things to do in life? Paloma replied that she'd already done all the other things in life.

A peaceful harmony, however, reigned in Paloma's house. Although her daughter-in-law loved to gossip about her and to complain about how she had to take care of all the household chores because Paloma wouldn't lift a finger, it so happened that Paloma's psychic retreat and Rodrigo's absence allowed this nineteen-year-old to be the head of the household. All the orders came from her. She ran the place. She took over. There was no clash between the two women; Paloma gave her daughter-in-law total power, and her daughter-in-law enjoyed that. In little or no time she stopped being a passionate pregnant teenager and became a bossy matron.

Word got to Rodrigo that Paloma was acting strange, that she was always tired, and that his daughter-in-law was now the mistress of the house. So Rodrigo decided to check this out and returned home for a four-day visit at the beginning of February. Instead of running to him with outstretched arms and at least ten contained hugs and kisses, Paloma hardly seemed to notice him. She was too busy getting ready to go out. She said she had an errand to run, that it was very important, and that she'd be back in a little while.

She walked in the direction of the market place and took the same bus she had taken before. This time she didn't have to travel as far. In a little village in the plains, two sisters were fighting. They both had long sharp nails and seemed to want to scratch each other's eyes out. They were also screeching like cats. The fight had begun over a lot of land six square feet big on which one of them had planted alfalfa for the pigs and watched the alfalfa grow until her sister had come to claim this portion of earth a bit bigger than a postage stamp. When Paloma arrived, they stopped screeching and fighting. "Which one of you is single?" Paloma asked. One of the she-cats raised her long-nailed hand and said, "I am." Paloma then followed her to her house, took the money, gave her the passport and instructions of what to do once she got to New York; send the passport back and fifty additional dollars a week for the next six months. They shook hands and said good-bye.

Three days later Rodrigo still hadn't left and Paloma dreamt she was flying. But Rodrigo was angry. He wanted his wife. He said he worked hard. He said he deserved what he wanted. He even threatened to abandon Paloma if her attitude didn't change. Paloma, in turn, gently replied that she was too nervous and too tired. The next day she could barely keep track of the time. She wondered whether it was two hours earlier or two hours later and kept asking her sex-starved husband what time it was. She said she was confused. She said she hadn't slept all night. Rodrigo left that day, threatening to return in a month, and that her attitude had better be different by then, or else.

She was in The Bronx. In a small factory. Four rows of sewing machines, side by side, and benches where four could fit but had to take turns lifting their elbows. There were women from every single country she had ever heard of. Bolivia, Colombia, Paraguay. They worked and talked all day, and each had their own transistor radio. They talked about clothes, makeup, men, husbands, and they also talked about themselves. The ones who had children brought their children to work. They ran up and down the narrow aisles between the benches. The men were on the other side of the wall. Everyone got fifteen cents per garment. They talked about birth control and how you had to pray to the moon if you didn't want a baby. They talked about the men on the other side of the wall. Some were worth marrying, others were going to succeed in this country, and like everywhere else there was one particular man that everyone was in love with and wanted. He was ambitious and handsome. He dressed well and smelled fine and even got a manicure every Saturday. His nails were clean and shiny. The women who didn't hate him called him an Adonis. The others hated him and called him the worst son of a whore that ever lived. Adalberto, that's what his name was, had broken some hearts in this factory. Those hearts were angry now. He'd even gotten five women on this side of the wall pregnant and obviously refused to

marry each and every one of them. Two of his children often
ran up and down the factory aisles.

At break time, one of her new friends pointed to Adalberto and said that that was him, and she fell madly in love
the minute she set eyes on him. Besides, she'd heard so much
about him that it was as if she'd already known him for two
weeks. Suddenly she no longer felt as lonely in this new country. For two weeks it had appeared empty, but now he was
here. She started loving every single corner of The Bronx
because The Bronx was where he worked and lived.

She in turn lived with three couples and four women in a
gloomy, windowless apartment near the factory. Her rent was
thirty dollars a week. The rest she began to spend on tight
sweaters, high-heeled shoes, tight stretch jeans, fancy
dresses, makeup, love witchcraft, anything to attract him.
She wondered how she had managed to live without his presence, without him being around. How boring life appeared up
to now. So this was love. She hardly ate. She was determined
to look like those girls on the covers of magazines. Every day
she had to punch in at the factory at six a.m. She woke at four
a.m. with a pounding, passionate heart. She was going to see
him! Another day of trying to make him notice her! Life was
worth living. Not even paradise could have competed with
that factory. Without hesitating, she would have turned paradise down. Adalberto. She wanted to be wherever Adalberto
was.

Every morning it took her forty-five minutes to get her
hair just right and another forty-five minutes to make her
face up. Deep green eyeshadow and lots of mascara. Her eyes
looked mysterious and big and wonderful. She also put lots of
foundation and powder on. The last touch was the blush, from
her cheekbone all the way up to her eyebrow. At five forty-five
a.m., she was ready to go to the factory.

The rest of the day was spent trying to get a glimpse of
Adalberto, as well as his attention. At break time, she'd look
for him in the crowd, discreetly sneak over to where he was,
call a girl friend over, begin a loud show-off conversation
about her past and her adventures, and finally burst out
laughing, for example, so he'd turn his head toward the
laughter, certainly wondering what that laughing was all
about. She'd then catch a glimpse of him in the corner of her
eye, and look away, or look down, feigning both indifference

and difference at the same time. One evening when she was punching out, he walked up to her and said that she had really caught his eye the day she started working here, but that he hadn't dared ask her out before. She was so pretty that she most probably belonged to another man. So if she was engaged or anything, it'd be O.K., he'd understand. He'd always like her though, he even thought he was in love with her. Would she like to go out with him? Of course she would! No, she meant, that, yes, she would. She meant it'd be nice.

They went out on Saturday. While they were dancing, he whispered in her ear that she should try being a model or an actress. She was way too pretty to be at the factory. She was the most beautiful woman in the factory. While they were sitting at the bar he said that he loved her dress. It was really sexy on her. He caressed her knee and told her she had spectacular legs. They ordered more beers. He caressed her thigh and told her that he'd noticed men looking at her while they were dancing and that he felt like walking up to them and punching them because he just couldn't stand to have a man setting eyes on her. In the car he continued talking about how jealous he was. He fondled her breasts and drew her closer to him, whispering I'm so jealous, I'm so jealous. I'm so scared that another man will take you away from me. I'll kill him, I swear. She thought she was in heaven. He lifted her skirt. He said the factory was just a stepping stone for him. He had many ideas. He said he was going to start his own business. He slipped her panty hose off, said he wanted to feel her skin, that was all. He said that his business was going to make him rich. In a month. He was going to begin in a month. The factory was just a stepping stone. In this country you have to be intelligent. If you don't have money you're nothing. He took her panties off. He said he had millions of ideas. He said he'd never been in love in his life until he first laid eyes on her. Then he laid down on top of her. There was barely enough room in the car, but there was enough room anyway. While they were making love, he kept begging her to marry him, to be his wife, forever. He said that if she didn't become his wife, he'd either kill himself or die.

The next day she announced her engagement at the factory and also talked about how horribly jealous he was. She loved it! The other women agreed that when you make a man jealous you've got him. She giggled and proudly continued talking about him. One of the jilted women slapped her and she slapped her back.

They spent Sunday together. A friend of Adalberto's lent him a dirty, stinky bachelor's apartment. Adalberto bought imitation champagne and wondered where they should spend their honeymoon. On Monday at the factory she talked about wedding dresses. On Monday night, once again, they made love in Adalberto's car. On Tuesday there was a new girl in the factory. Perhaps she had tighter jeans, higher heels, and tighter sweaters. Perhaps she was seventeen. But the important thing was that she was new. She'd also laugh out loud and pretend Adalberto wasn't around. On Tuesday night in the car, Adalberto told her that the new girl wasn't half as pretty as she was. He then proceeded to slip off her panty hose and panties. On Wednesday she caught him talking to the new girl at break time. She screeched and tried to scratch her face. Adalberto had to separate them. When they were alone, he repeated that she was indeed the love of his life, but they simply have to wait a while before they got married, a man like him needed more room, he had millions of ideas and was going to start a new business next month. Since she didn't get the point, he said he didn't deserve her. He almost cried. Then he cried. She tried to comfort him. Everything would be all right. Adalberto didn't think so. He complained about being too jealous. They made love. Then Adalberto got angry. He accused her of flirting with some other man in the factory. She swore it wasn't true, but he hit her and pushed her around. She cried. On Thursday morning she announced that they'd quarreled. All her co-workers were interested and wanted to hear more about it. She cried and she cried. He started ignoring her. Maybe this was just a lovers' quarrel. He was so jealous! She waited. Then she slowly became friends with the other jilted ones. Two weeks later the new girl was also a jilted girl. She cried. Adalberto had promised to marry her! He'd talked about how jealous he was! Said he'd never had this passionate feeling for a woman in his whole life! He even threatened to commit suicide! She joined the club. They hated all the new girls that came to the factory. At least they hated them until the engagement was called off. They also hated Adalberto. But they continued aching for him. He'd been working there for two years, but the factory was just a stepping stone. Next month he'd start his own business. He said he was intelligent and had millions of ideas.

Paloma told Rodrigo that she never wanted to be with a man again. Men were liars and traitors. Rodrigo pushed her around and hit her and tried to force her. Nothing would do. She said she hated men. He finally left the next day and threatened to return in a month and that her attitude had better be different by then, or else.

Word started getting to Paloma unexpectedly. She even had to turn down some of the women who came to her with their requests. But whenever she had dreamt she was flying, she usually accepted their money. Only cash. Meanwhile, in the capital, Rodrigo was surprised to encounter so many traveling women named Paloma Sánchez. At first it had only happened once a month, then twice a month, now once a week some common-looking Paloma Sánchez would be traveling to New York. And they never returned. Nobody expected them to anyway. They left and disappeared into the American woodwork. So far he had counted fifteen women by the name of Paloma Sánchez. This, combined with the hard time he was having at home, most likely gave him the idea that Paloma Sánchez, his Paloma Sánchez, was probably not the only fish in the sea. There even seemed to be a surplus of her namesakes!

So, Rodrigo ended up taking a mistress by the name of Gladys. Perhaps Gladys wasn't as pretty as his Paloma Sánchez, but she was sweet and available and always eager to see him. He had grown weary of his distant wife. Not only that, but Gladys was photogenic. She looked beautiful on a developed photograph, which allowed Rodrigo to satisfy his lifelong dream: everlasting proof of what a woman of his had once been. He even wanted to have children with Gladys. Just so the hypothetical children and grandchildren could admire her photos in the future.

Back home, Paloma could barely keep up. At least the flying didn't make her as nervous anymore. It was even beginning to bore her. The taking off, the landing, those people in uniform with their questions, ready to send you back if you make the slightest mistake, she felt like an expert. She was more than used to landing in New York and disappearing into the woodwork, as they say. At four a.m. she was putting blue eye shadow on her eyelids, at five a.m. she was sleeping in a

little bed in a little room, either on Park Avenue, or on Fifth
Avenue, on on Central Park South or West, at six a.m. she
was mowing lawns in Montauk, Long Island, at seven a.m.
she was painting a house in Poughkeepsie, New York, an
hour later she was madly in love, rushing to have a cup of coffee with a new love, or she was missing her husband, or she
was missing the love she'd left behind to come here and make
lots of money. It's terrible to miss someone. The whole country seems empty if that one person isn't around. She'd then be
hating her lover and saying terrible things about him and
wishing he were sick, old, in a wheelchair, paralyzed. She
made friends with all the women who'd loved him and
together they'd wonder if he'd ever really marry. By mid-
morning she'd be reading letters from her children; she had
forty children now and six at her breast, seven on her lap. She
was carrying three or four different children in her womb, but
she went to a clinic and got rid of one because she had been
forced in Brooklyn. This kind of thing never happened in her
land, to get rid of a child. Before this she'd never even heard
of it. At lunchtime she was either having a meat-less, salt-
less, sugar-less, sodium-less, and cholesterol-free meal for her
figure, or trying on tight jeans in the stores of Queens, or gossiping about the people who stayed back home, the ones who
tried coming to New York and had failed, the ones who had
made it and already had a car and a refrigerator, the ones
who hadn't made it and had gone to jail, either here or there.
Or she was aching for some new man and she was convinced
that it was really love this time. Or she was still aching for
that same one, who was now engaged for the fifteenth time
since she'd arrived. Why was he so handsome? She loved him
so and wished he were dead right now. Or perhaps he'd catch
that dreadful disease that the buses and the subway and the
radio talked about all the time. On Wednesday evening, she
was unfaithful to her husband then she missed him terribly
because he was such a good man. Then, after having finished
painting the house in Poughkeepsie, she started taking the
paint off her hair with turpentine. The next day she lost her
index finger to a lawnmower. The needle from one of the
sewing machines went right through her thumb. On Friday
she had a date and she was passionately in love. She bought a
party dress and high heels and fancy stockings. And she
cleaned offices until twelve midnight. Now she was flying

again. Her husband was waiting for her in New York and she
hadn't seen him in three years. She was only twenty years
old. Then she died. It happened suddenly. After having
cleaned the lawyer's office, she was waiting for the train. It
happened in the subway. Four men killed her. It hurt. They
named her Jane Doe and it was cold in the morgue. Nobody to
claim her body. Then she became an alcoholic. Then she was a
drug addict. Then she met that horrible man who promised
her the world. All she had to do was carry a suitcase from
New York to Miami. One day they caught her. The suitcase
was full of flour. They put her in prison. Oh, she was so happy
the day her husband got his green card! That meant they
could lead normal lives. No more fear of getting caught by
immigration and sent back. Out of the woodwork. No more
hiding.

Paloma's husband left her for Gladys. She hardly noticed
he was going. As a matter of fact she was a bit relieved; a
peaceful harmony reigned in the house when he was absent.
But she didn't even have time to wonder how she felt now
that she was an abandoned woman. It was Tuesday. On Tues-
days she rushed to the post office. Her passport always came
back on Tuesday.

She asked Rodrigo if she could leave for New York. She
said she wanted to start a new life there. Her daughter-in-law
had turned out to be an excellent matron, so they didn't need
her at home. Paloma even spoke English now. Rodrigo didn't
seem to mind, he was too busy admiring and showing everyone the latest photographs of Gladys.

They said good-bye at the airport. Not that he accompanied her there, but that's where he worked. His last words
were, "I'll probably never see you again." Paloma boarded an
Eastern Airlines flight to Miami. She was thirty years old,
three times a grandmother, and as beautiful as ever. She had
money, she spoke English, she dressed well. And she knew
customs and immigration by heart for having gone through
there so so many times. She also knew what the questions
would be and how to answer them. They'd ask her to sign her
name several times, but that was her signature. Anyway, she
had nothing to fear, she had a passport, quite a bit of money,
and a visa.

Passport. Your name? How long do you plan to stay?
Why? Where? How much money are you bringing? He opened

her passport and looked at her photo then looked at her then back at the photo then back at her and smiled. He asked, "Amiga, do you think we're blind?" He called a co-worker of his and exclaimed, "Hey, Joe, look at this! Our amiga here must think we're blind. What do you think?" Joe thought out loud, "I think we've got one here." They both asked her if she really thought they'd fall for that. They had thousands of her kind leaking in through here and they had, what they called, the professional eye. "I can spot them from a mile away," Joe said. "Amiga, it's not that easy to sneak into the United States," the other one added. "Did you really think we'd fall for this?" he asked and slapped the passport. "You're way too pretty."

They showed her to a small waiting area, offered her coffee, then dinner. She waited hours. Some of her people were also in there. Waiting. Waiting for the plane that would take them back. It was hard getting into the United States, they agreed. You couldn't just slip by the customs officials like that. They had the "eye." Even the men cried. They'd be put in jail the minute they got back. But Paloma's eyes remained dry. "Aren't you upset?" someone asked her. "No. There are sixty-seven of me here already," she replied.